The Sailor's Kiss

A NOVELLA

Journeys of the Heart

PROPER HISTORICAL ROMANCES

The Sailor's Kiss

SHAELA KAY

 Blue Water Books

Other books in this series

A Heart Made of Indigo
Scoundrel In Disguise

Published by Blue Water Books
Richland, WA

Cover photo © Period Images
Cover design © Blue Water Books

© 2017 Shaela Kay Odd
Visit the author at www.shaelakay.com

This book is a work of fiction. While great care has been taken to ensure historical accuracy of dates and locations, characters and events in this book are products of the author's imagination and are represented fictitiously. Any likeness to any person, living or dead, is purely coincidental.

For my children

Chapter 1

September 1809
Wallasey, England

"Thank you, Mrs. Whidlow. Come again soon."

Elizabeth glanced at the clock for the hundredth time as she escorted her customer to the door. It was nearly six in the evening, and at last it was time to close the shop. She turned the latch and flipped the sign in the window. Quickly, she swept and tidied the front of the store. Abram Wilson prided himself on having the neatest general store in Wallasey, and he would not be pleased if he found that his daughter had left it in shambles.

Setting the broom in its place behind the counter, Elizabeth slipped out the back entrance. A cool autumn breeze blew across her face as she secured the door behind her. Her pulse quickened, and she smiled to herself. *Stephen will be waiting.*

Wrapping her shawl more tightly around her shoulders, she hurried along the path leading north out of town. Wallasey was a small village on the tip of the Wirral Peninsula, near Liverpool, England. The town was nearly an island, being bordered on three sides by water: the Irish Sea on the north, the River Mersey to the east, and a creek to the south known as Wallasey Pool. It boasted nearly four miles of beautiful coastline, and the sandy beaches were a favorite haunt of Elizabeth's. She glanced up at the sky as she made her way down the shoreline trail. The sun would not set for more than an hour, but already the temperature was dropping. She shivered as she climbed the small hill overlooking the beach.

As soon as she came to the top of the knoll, she saw him – sitting on a large driftwood log with his back to her. Stephen Jones had broad shoulders and a muscular back from working in the warehouses along Bridgewater Street, across the river in Liverpool. Sandy blonde hair covered his head, which was bent over something he held in his hands. As Elizabeth drew nearer, she could hear his deep voice singing softly.

Our anchor we'll weigh,
And our sails we will set.
Goodbye, fare-ye-well,
Goodbye, fare-ye-well.
The friends we are leaving,
We leave with regret,
Hurrah, my boys, we're homeward bound.

It was an old sailing song, no doubt one he had learned at his father's knee. Elizabeth slipped undetected behind him and placed her hands over his eyes.

"Och, I'd know those dainty hands anywhere. 'Tis my darling Eleanor!"

"Eleanor!" Elizabeth cried, pulling her hands back. But

Stephen laughed, putting his work away. He stood and turned around to face her.

"Only joshing you, Beth. 'Course I knew 'twas you."

Pulling her into an embrace, Stephen buried his face in her hair. Elizabeth closed her eyes, resting her cheek against his chest, breathing deeply. He smelled of salt and wind and fresh cut wood. *This is where I belong*, she thought.

Stephen held her close for a few minutes before letting go. He clasped her hand in one of his own, and held it tightly as they stepped around the fallen tree and continued up the beach. The wind was stronger along the tide line, and Elizabeth huddled against him for warmth.

"What were you working on before I came?" she asked.

"Just a trinket for Caleb. The lad was crying over the wooden horse he saw in your father's shop last week, so I thought I'd try my hand at carving one."

He produced the rough wooden figure from his pocket for her inspection. It was no bigger than her hand, but Elizabeth could already see the head and tail emerging from the block of weathered wood.

"He will love it," she said with a smile, handing it back to him.

Stephen grinned. He had a plain face, with a large, lopsided mouth and an over-sized nose. Nobody who saw him would consider him handsome, but Elizabeth did not care. She and Stephen had known each other nearly their whole lives, their friendship dating back to the early years of childhood when the outward appearance of your playmate mattered not at all.

Stephen, on the other hand, had always been aware of

Elizabeth's beauty. Light hair, fair skin, and a ready smile made Elizabeth Wilson very pretty in her own right, but it was her eyes that set her apart from the crowd. They were large and round, full of compassion and kindness, with a brightness born from the joy she received in serving those around her. Stephen thought their rich brown hue was never more beautiful than when she was smiling at him. Her whole face lit up, and in those moments he realized how truly fortunate he was to have earned not only her friendship, but also her love.

They walked in companionable silence for some time, enjoying the cry of the gulls and the crash of the waves along the shore. Elizabeth's hand was snug inside of Stephen's larger one, and she sighed contentedly.

"Your birthday is next week," she ventured after awhile.

Stephen merely nodded.

"What would you like as a gift?" she prodded.

He looked down at her, a mischievous glint in his eye. "How about a kiss?"

"Stephen Jones!" Elizabeth cried, laughing. Bright pink patches appeared on her cheeks, and there was an eager sparkle in her eyes. He laughed right back at her.

"Now, don't pretend to be affronted, Beth," he teased. "That's what I plan on giving you for your birthday, you know. Why can't I expect the same?"

Elizabeth could not hide her smile, but she tossed her head in a show of dignity. "Well, perhaps when we are engaged, Mr. Jones," she said airily.

"Engaged! Why, Beth, we've been as good as engaged these last three years, at least!"

"Have you spoken with my father?"

"Now, 'Lizbeth, why should I be speaking to your father? You know as well as I he'd love to have me for a son-in-law."

"Yes, but is it not customary to ask permission of the father of one's intended?"

"Aye, but not for the likes of you and me, Beth. How long have we known each other now?"

Elizabeth glanced up at him. His look was gentle, but his eyes were teasing. "Since we were four years old," she said.

"Nigh on fifteen years then, Beth. And I've been sweet on you since the moment we met."

She laughed. "You have not!"

"Haven't I? Och, I remember it like 'twas yesterday. You were standing by the side of the road in a pretty blue dress..."

"Crying my eyes out, because Jebediah Howell splashed mud on my skirt."

Stephen chuckled. "Aye."

"You wanted to know what I was so upset about, and when I told you, *you* jumped in the mud yourself, just to show me there was nothing to cry about!"

They were each of them laughing now, but the cheerful sound blew away on the wind the moment it left their lips.

"I was fresh off the boat from Ireland when we met, Beth. You were the first friend I had here."

"After the mud incident, I was the only one who *wanted* to be your friend," she teased.

He laughed, giving her hand a squeeze, and Elizabeth smiled. The sun was beginning to set, and the gathering clouds above the horizon were streaked with scarlet and pink. Stephen led her down the shore to a large tree, uprooted by some ancient storm and bleached nearly white from its years in the salty air. Stepping over to the lee side of it, he pulled Elizabeth down onto the sand, so she was sitting beside him. He put his arm around her, and she leaned her head on his shoulder, gazing out over the ocean. They were silent for a time, each lost in their memories of the years they had shared together.

"I haven't spoken with your father because I've got nothing to offer you, Beth. Not yet."

"I know."

"But you know I want to marry you."

"Yes."

They spoke quietly, huddled together against the tree, watching the waves rush against the shore. They beat mercilessly against the sandy coastline, frothing angrily as they crashed over each other. Stephen shifted nervously.

"And you, Beth? Do *you* want to marry *me?*"

"You know the answer to that, Stephen."

"But you could have any young man in the village, Beth. You're beautiful, and witty, and kind... Are you sure you want to marry a nobody like me?

Elizabeth lifted her head and looked at him. Stephen was squinting at the water, deliberately avoiding her gaze. She waited patiently, knowing that he would eventually look at her. When he could stand the silence no longer, he glanced down at her, his eyes full of uncertainty. Elizabeth reached up and cupped his cheek, ensuring that he would not look away, and gazed squarely into his hazel-gray eyes.

"Stephen Jones, I love you with all my heart. There is no one else I would rather marry than you." A smile tugged at her mouth, and she added, "Mud and all."

Stephen's anxious expression relaxed, and a smile stretched across his face. With the wind mussing his hair, Elizabeth thought that he really looked almost handsome. She knew it troubled him at times – his plainness, that is. But she did not care. He knew her better than anyone else, and he loved her all the same. She trusted him. She felt safe with him. She knew she could rely on him, no matter what, and those qualities were far more important to Elizabeth than a handsome face. She rested her head once more on his shoulder, content to be with the man she loved.

The first fat drops of rain were just beginning to fall as Stephen and Elizabeth hurried down the lane leading to her home. The storm came on swiftly, and stole the light a full twenty minutes before sundown. The young couple had to run most of the way home from the beach in order to arrive before nightfall. They were winded but exultant, as only young lovers can be.

"Thank you for the walk, Stephen," Elizabeth said, somewhat out of breath. He grinned.

"Anytime, Miss Wilson," he teased. He leaned down so his lips brushed against her ear. "And think about that kiss," he murmured. Flashing her a lopsided smile, he dashed out into the darkening night.

Elizabeth's cheeks burned, and she took a few deep breaths to compose herself before opening the front door. Smoothing back her tangled tresses, she turned the knob and stepped into the house.

Abram and Mary Wilson had a snug little home in the western part of town known as The Village. It was a residential district, with only a few church spires punctuating the sea of modest rooftops. Elizabeth was their youngest child and the only one still left at home – her older sister Charlotte having married and moved to Liverpool, and her brother, Henry, employed with a family in London.

"Elizabeth, at last!" her mother cried, standing from her seat before the fire.

"I am sorry, Mama. I lost track of time, and the rain came on so suddenly–"

"Hush, my child. I am not angry; I was only a bit worried."

Elizabeth relaxed. She hung her shawl on the screen before the fire, careful to ensure it was a safe distance from the flames. Her mother sat back down and resumed her knitting.

"Where is Papa?" Elizabeth asked, looking around.

Her mother sighed. "He is at St. Hillary's this evening. Father Morrison is not faring well."

The old priest had suffered ill health for many years, and his death had been expected for some time. A few parish members, including Abram Wilson, had been called to the priest's home along with the doctor earlier in the evening.

"I do not know if he will pull through again," her mother said as Elizabeth sat beside her. "He will be sorely missed when he is gone." She dabbed at her eyes, and Elizabeth patted her gently. "There now, why am I carrying on so? There will be time enough for tears, I am sure, in the future." She shifted in her seat, shaking off her melancholy. "You were certainly bright-eyed when you returned home. How is Stephen this evening?"

"He is well."

"His birthday is soon, is it not?"

"Yes, next week."

"Have you decided what to give him?"

"No," Elizabeth said, turning pink as she thought of his request.

"Why, Elizabeth!" her mother cried. "Why do you blush? Has he asked for a wife for his birthday?"

"Mama!"

"Come now, why should you look at me like that? Is that not what you have decided between you?"

Elizabeth nearly choked on her embarrassment. "Whether we have or not does not signify, for he has not yet spoken to Papa."

"Tsh! That is of no consequence. You know perfectly well we would be very pleased to have Stephen for a son-in-law. He is a fine, hard-working young man, and you could do far worse. Although," she frowned thoughtfully, "does he plan to work at the warehouse forever?"

Elizabeth hesitated. "I do not know. He has not spoken to me of anything else, so I would assume so. Does it bother you that Stephen is merely a laborer?"

"No, my dear. As I said before, he is a hard worker and I know he can provide for you. But a laborer does not make very much money – how can he possibly afford a house? I would rather see him promoted to foreman, or even owner of his own warehouse before you marry."

"Mama! We are not even engaged."

"*Yet*," her mother added with a sly smile.

Elizabeth was saved from further distress by the opening of the front door. A cold gust of wind blew in with her father, and Elizabeth hurried to shut the door behind him.

"Thank you, Beth," he said, shaking off his great coat and doffing his beaver skin hat. Tiny droplets of freezing water pelted Elizabeth's skin as he removed the soaking articles, handing them to her. She set his hat on a chair near the fire, and replaced the shawl on the screen with her father's coat.

Mary Wilson stood nearby, anxiously waiting for her husband to acknowledge her. When he at last turned to face her, he smiled and nodded.

"Oh, Abram!" she cried, collapsing on the sofa.

"There, there, Mary," he soothed, sitting beside her and taking her hand. "Why do you carry on so? Father Morrison has pulled through once again, as I told you he would. It will take more than pneumonia to carry off that old soul."

"But you were so somber when you left! And he is getting so old," she mumbled, blowing her nose into her handkerchief.

"Yes, but he is not gone yet."

"Could you not have sent me word? I have been all of a dither since dinnertime."

"Come now, Mary, you know Father Morrison only employs the Edmonds' girl. How could I have sent you word without leaving his side?"

Mary sniffed. "If we kept a manservant ourselves, I could have sent *him* to fetch your news."

Closing his eyes, Abram sighed. "Mary, we have been through this – we cannot afford to keep a manservant *and* Annie Prewett. And what good would it do to have someone to keep the carriage if there is no one to help you in the kitchen?"

Mary sniffed again, and Abram turned to his daughter. "Ah, Elizabeth," he said, changing the subject, "I am glad you are home. I was afraid you may have been caught in the storm on your way back from the store."

"It was not raining when I closed the shop, Papa."

"No, but you do not always come straight home now, do you?" he teased.

Elizabeth smiled, and her father chuckled.

"How is young Jones faring?"

"He is well, Papa."

"Almost nineteen now, isn't he?"

"His birthday is next week," Mary chimed in, "and I was just telling Elizabeth that *I* think–"

"I believe I shall help Annie get supper on the table," Elizabeth broke in, excusing herself.

She fled the room before she heard another word her mother said. Whether her parents spoke of Elizabeth and Stephen's marriage as absolute did not concern her, but she would not be embarrassed at having it spoken in such certain terms before her face.

Supper was quiet and cozy. Elizabeth helped to clear the table afterward, while Annie, their maid, washed the dishes. She could hear her parents in the other room, discussing the approaching nuptials of a neighbor's daughter with mild interest. Rather than face the knowing glances and ill-concealed attempts at subtlety, Elizabeth opted to help in the kitchen until there was absolutely nothing else for her to do. Then, instead of joining her parents in the parlor, she told Annie she was tired and stole up the stairs to

11

seek refuge in bed.

Safe within the walls of her own room, Elizabeth lit a candle and slipped into her nightdress. She shivered. Crawling under the covers, she reached for the worn leather volume sitting on her bedside table. It was a collection of William Shakespeare's *Sonnets*, but on the blank pages at the end of the book, Stephen had penned a few verses of his own. She leafed through the book until she reached the very end. Stephen's untidy scrawl was still legible, though the paper was faded and worn.

Neither storm, nor wind, nor rushing sea
Can remove the love from within my heart.
And in my arms, ever circled be
My darling Beth, ne'er again to part.

Her girlish heart fluttered as she read the words he had written. They were only simple phrases and expressions, but they were written for *her.*

Smiling to herself, she lifted the much-loved volume to her mouth and kissed it softly. Someday soon, it would be Stephen's lips, not just his words, that she pressed against her own.

Chapter 2

Stephen's home was located on the other side of Wallasey, in a small community known as Poulton. Despite the fact that he ran most of the way, Stephen was soaked through by the time he arrived at the little house he shared with his mother and younger siblings. A light was burning in the window, and Stephen knew his mother would be waiting up for him.

Unlatching the door as quietly as he could, he slipped through the narrow opening, trying not to invite the storm inside with him. As he suspected, his mother, Lucy, was sitting at the crude wooden table in the center of the room. He glanced toward the corner, where his younger brother and sister were sleeping on their bed, under a large patchwork quilt which they shared.

Shutting the door quietly behind him, Stephen removed his threadbare jacket and hung it on a chair near the fire. He placed his muddy boots next to the hearth and sat down across from his mother. She stood the moment he was seated.

"You'll catch your death of cold in them damp clothes," she warned, retrieving a small crock of soup from where it was warming on the hearth. The sharpness in her voice exaggerated her Irish brogue, and Stephen felt a stab of guilt at her words.

"I'm sorry, Mam," he offered. "I know the storm makes you nervous. But I'm home now."

Lucy said nothing, only set the bowl in front of him. She took a small piece of bread from the cupboard and handed it to him, along with a spoon. Stephen started to eat, and his mother sat down again.

"Out with 'Lizbeth again, were you?"

Stephen nodded, and she sniffed.

"She must have the patience of a saint, waitin' 'round for you to propose."

Lucy threw her bait and waited, watching her son shrewdly. He gave no reply.

"Have you not spoken about it 'twixt yourselves? She's eighteen, m'boy. She'll be wantin' a family 'fore long."

"Eighteen is still young."

"Old enough to be movin' on in life. Why, your father and I had been married two years already by the time I was eighteen! And you was toddlin' all o'er Dublin as well."

Stephen merely shrugged and continued eating his soup. Lucy threw up her hands in exasperation. "M'boy, if you're not intent on marryin' the lass, what are you about?"

"What sort of question is that?"

"The kind that wants answerin', son."

"You know how I feel about her."

"Do I? I thought you loved her."

"I do love her."

"Then why have you not spoken?"

Stephen studied her for a moment. "I'll be nineteen next week."

Lucy blanched.

Stephen finished his supper, then took his dishes to the washbasin. After scrubbing them clean, he set them back in their places and turned to face his mother.

She was looking away from him, both arms wrapped tightly around her waist, as if holding herself together.

"Mam," Stephen said gently, pulling a chair out to sit beside her. "We've been through this. We agreed that when I turned nineteen, you'd–"

"Don't, don't!" his mother whispered, tears spilling from her eyes. "I canna bear it, Stephen. First your father, then you... what about Caleb? Will he run off an' leave me as well?"

Stephen grasped her hand, but she withdrew it. He sighed.

"Da didn't leave you," he said. "He was a sailor when you married him."

"Aye, and 'twas the most foolish thing I ever did! Marryin' a sailor..." Suddenly she turned, fixing her eyes intently on his face.

"'Lizbeth Wilson won't marry a sailor," she snapped.

Stephen flinched. "She loves me. She'll marry me."

"Marry you, only to watch you sail away from her, mayhaps forever?"

"She'll wait."

"Wait?" Lucy laughed cynically. "M'boy, that lass'll wait for no one. Not with her pretty face. If you run off to sea, she'll be married in a trice."

Stephen sat back, rubbing a hand across his face. His mother wore a look of triumph, and he sighed.

"You promised, Mam. You promised that when I turned nineteen, you wouldn't stop me from putting to sea. I could have gone years ago. I could have been a cabin boy at fourteen if Da–"

He caught himself, but not soon enough. His mother turned away.

"If Da hadn't died," he mumbled.

Lucy Jones sat stiffly beside him, her shoulders shaking slightly from suppressing her sobs. She was only thirty-seven, but grief and hardship had turned her prematurely gray, and deep creases lined her face. She was thin, but tall – nearly as tall as Stephen, who stood just shy of six feet.

"I've already spoken with Captain O'Malley down at the Liverpool docks. He's putting to sea in a few week's time and is looking for sailors. He's willing to take me on."

Lucy remained silent.

"'Tis in my blood, Mam. I've been dreaming of the sea since I was a lad. You know that." He shifted uncomfortably in his seat, but still his mother said nothing. He knew what would happen. She would sulk, and cry, and make him feel guilty for wanting to leave them, until he finally relented and bent to her will.

But not this time.

Stephen stood abruptly, his chair scraping loudly across the floor as he shoved it backward. His eyes flashed as he looked down at her.

"In the last five years, since Da died, have you ever heard me complain? Pulling double shifts at the warehouse to help put food on the table, did I ever think to leave? Have you ever known me to put me own wishes above the needs of you or Sophy or Caleb?"

16

"Quiet, Stephen, you'll wake the children!"

But he continued, not bothering to keep his voice down. Like his mother, his brogue grew thicker the more animated he became. "I'm a man now, Mam. And I've got to think of me own future. I won't turn me back on me family, but I won't sit here and let me dreams die either, just because–"

"Stephen?" a sleepy voice called from the corner. Lucy shot Stephen a withering look, then hurried over to where her younger son was rubbing the sleep from his eyes.

"Hush now, 'tis alright."

"I heard Stephen shouting."

"I'm sorry, Caleb," Stephen said, joining them. "Mam and I were just talking about me going to sea."

"Stephen!"

"What? He has a right to know."

"We're not talkin' about anythin'. Nothin' has been decided," his mother hissed.

"Are you really going to be a sailor?" the young boy asked.

"No, he's not."

"Yes, Caleb, I am," Stephen said, ignoring the scowl on his mother's face. "But I'm not leaving tonight, so you've nothing to worry about just now."

"When will you go?"

"In a few weeks. Maybe a month. When we sail depends upon the tide, and the weather."

"I want to go with you."

Stephen's look softened, but his mother glared at him. "You see? D'you see what you've done? Now Caleb will get it into his head that he's got to run off to sea after his brother, and then you'll both be killed, and Sophronia and I will be left in the poorhouse with no one to look after us and no one to care what happens to us at all!"

She dissolved into tears beside her sons, and Stephen took her in his arms. His twelve-year-old sister, Sophy, had awoken, and she sat watching them, wide-eyed and silent.

"Och, Mam," Stephen sighed. "I'm sorry. But I've got to do this."

"My boy," his mother moaned. "My son."

Stephen held her as she cried, rocking her back and forth like a baby; like he had when his father had been lost at sea. Gradually her sobs subsided, and at last she drew away, wiping her tear-streaked face on her apron.

"Mam?" Caleb ventured after awhile.

"'Tis alright, son. Go to sleep."

"But is it true? Will Stephen be leaving us?"

"We'll talk of it in the mornin'. Get some sleep. You too, Sophy," she insisted.

The children burrowed back under the covers, and Stephen retreated to the far side of the room while his mother tucked them in again. He knelt down to bank the fire, and by the time he was finished, she was standing behind him, her arms folded across her chest. He sighed.

"I don't want to argue anymore, Mam."

"Nor do I."

"Then you won't raise a fuss when I sign the contract with Captain O'Malley next week."

It was not a question. Lucy turned stiffly and stalked to her bed across the room. A worn bedsheet hung from a rope tied across the ceiling to allow her some privacy, but at the moment it was pulled aside. She turned to face him, and even across the room he could see her eyes flashing.

"I won't try to talk you out of it, if that's what you're askin'. 'Tis plain you haven't a care for me own feelin's."

"Mam..."

"I said I won't stop you, Stephen," she snapped. "But mark me words: Elizabeth Wilson might."

Chapter 3

Elizabeth knew just what to give Stephen for his birthday. With the arrival of the autumn rains came cooler temperatures, and she had noticed that his jacket was nearly in pieces. A warm winter coat was precisely what he needed, and Elizabeth set to work on it immediately.

Though her father's store carried bolts of beautiful broadcloth, she knew that Stephen would feel out of place in a coat made of such fine material. He was a simple, humble man, and Elizabeth determined to make his coat out of sturdy, homespun wool. She chose a gray wool with flecks of white and black from the modest selection available, and a warm, red flannel for the lining.

"Not out with Stephen?" her mother asked when she arrived home at half-past six the next evening.

"No, I must work on his birthday present."

Elizabeth showed her mother the fabric and explained her idea. Mary nodded in approval.

"A marvelous plan, Beth. He was in the store with his younger brother last week, and I noticed that the jacket he had on would barely keep a beggar warm."

Taking one of her father's old winter coats from the closet, Elizabeth sat down to work out a pattern. Stephen was taller and larger built than Abram Wilson, but she did her best to make appropriate adjustments, and by the end of the evening she had all the pieces cut. She folded the material neatly and stacked it on a chair near the foot of her bed, ready to be sewn the following day.

But when she awoke the next morning, she found that instead of devoting the day to piecing the coat together, she would be managing the counter at her father's shop.

"All day?" she asked over breakfast, her stomach sinking.

"Elizabeth," Abram looked at her reprovingly, "Father Morrison is still very weak. Your mother and I are going to help at the manse, and we are counting on you to do your part."

"Yes, Papa."

"There's a good girl. Now run along with you – it is nearly time to open the store."

Elizabeth carefully bundled the pieces of fabric together and slipped them under her cloak. She kissed her parents goodbye and set out into the misty morning.

Wilson's Mercantile was located in the northeast corner of town, along one of the more busy thoroughfares of Wallasey. Sandwiched between a seamstress' shop and the local blacksmith, Abram Wilson's store was one of the local hubs to which the townsfolk gathered. It had a wide front porch laid out with smooth wooden planks, and large paned-glass windows sat on either side of the front door. Inside, the walls were lined with shelves, and the floor was covered in casks, crates, barrels, and boxes. Tables laden with household necessities dotted the room: bolts of brightly colored fabric, sacks of ten-penny nails, teakettles, frying pans, hand tools, and children's toys. Bins of potatoes and apples, sacks of flour and grain; almost anything you would ever need could be found there.

Elizabeth was determined to work on Stephen's coat whenever there was a lull in the day's business. But the September storm had awoken in the community the realization that winter was just around the corner, and she was busy from the moment she first opened the door.

One pleasant aspect about spending her days at the store is that Elizabeth saw her friends and neighbors more often. Mrs. Long inquired after her mother, Raymond Blewett came to announce that his wife had given birth to another son, and Elizabeth helped her friend Rebecca pick out some fabric for a new dress.

At half past one, she finally had a chance to sit down. Her neck and back were aching from lifting and carrying various items to fill the orders of customers. Glad to be off her feet, she pulled out a needle and thread and set to work on Stephen's coat. She had nearly finished stitching the seam on one of the sleeves when the bell above the door tinkled softly.

It was Stephen Jones, with his younger sister Sophy. Elizabeth stuffed the fabric behind the counter and stood abruptly, flushing in agitation. "Good day, Mr. Jones. Hello, Sophy."

Stephen's eyes twinkled merrily in response to the formality of her greeting. "Afternoon, Miss Wilson. I, ah, hope we're not interrupting anything?"

"No, no, not at all," Elizabeth said, forcing a laugh. "What can I do for you today?"

"Mam wants a pound of sugar," Sophy said brightly.

"Aye, and a sack of wheat. Might as well take a pound of coffee, too."

Sophy wandered over to look at the bolts of fabric on a nearby table, but she kept sneaking glances at the brightly colored candy jars sitting high up on a shelf. As Elizabeth measured out the coffee and poured it into the grinder, Stephen leaned against the counter, watching her.

"Did you hear about Father Morrison?" she asked nervously.

"Aye. Is he any better?"

"I believe so. Papa says he will pull through."

"Is your father there with him today?"

"Yes, he is."

"Pity," Stephen said. "I was hoping to have a word with him."

Elizabeth's stomach lurched. Why would Stephen need to speak with her father? She glanced up from the grinder and Stephen winked at her. With trembling hands, Elizabeth poured the ground coffee into a small paper sack and pulled out the sugar.

"Will he be home this evening?" Stephen asked.

"I believe so, yes," came her shaky reply.

He grinned.

"How much sugar did your mother need, Sophy?" Elizabeth called, trying to compose herself.

"A pound," the girl replied, fingering the folds of a blue-striped calico.

Elizabeth used the sugar nips to break off pieces from the large, white cone. She weighed the broken pieces on the scale and dropped them into another bag. Placing it next to the coffee, she nodded at the sacks of grain near the front door.

"The wheat is over there – we have red and white both."

Flashing her a smile, Stephen picked up a large sack and slung it onto his shoulder with ease. "Thank you. I'll be back to settle the account with your father in a few days," he said. "Come, Sophy."

His sister took the small brown bags from the counter and turned to follow him out of the shop.

"Wait!"

They stopped in the doorway and looked back. Stepping around the counter, Elizabeth reached up and pulled a jar of striped candy off the shelf. Sophy's eyes brightened.

Placing the jar on the counter, Elizabeth pulled out two small sticks of peppermint and wrapped them in a bit of waxed paper. She smiled, holding the parcel out to Sophy.

"Will you share this with Caleb?" she asked.

Nodding vigorously, Sophy took the candy and grinned.

"Thanks, Beth," Stephen murmured, his eyes full of warmth. Elizabeth inclined her head, and he ducked outside. "See you tonight!" he called.

The door closed behind them and Elizabeth returned to her seat. Smiling to herself, she pulled out the pieces of wool and began sewing again. Perhaps the coat would be a betrothal gift instead of a birthday one.

True to his word, Stephen stopped by the Wilson's home that evening after supper. Elizabeth answered the door, nervous but excited, and showed him into the parlor. Stephen appeared to be just as anxious as she was, and her mother gave Elizabeth a knowing look when she returned to the kitchen afterwards.

"We had better start making your trousseau, my dear," she hinted.

Though she was supposed to be darning stockings with her mother, Elizabeth was distracted the entire time Stephen and her father were talking. When the parlor door at last opened, she hurried over to meet them.

"Stop by again soon, Stephen," her father was saying.

Stephen smiled and nodded, then turned to Elizabeth. His eyes were bright with excitement, and Elizabeth's blood pounded in her ears.

"I shall see him out, Papa," she offered.

Abram Wilson chuckled, murmuring something about the joys of youth as he disappeared down the hallway.

Elizabeth threw a shawl around her shoulders as she and Stephen stepped outside. The stars shone brightly in the clear night sky, and the chilly air was filled with the chorus of crickets.

Stephen stepped off the porch and turned to face her, leaning against the baluster. Elizabeth came to stand beside him, drawing the woolen shawl tightly around her for warmth. She tipped her head up, gazing at the crescent moon hanging in the inky sky.

"You're even prettier by moonlight, Beth," Stephen said softly.

Elizabeth blushed. She felt suddenly shy, and it unsettled her. Stephen was her best friend, and she knew his feelings for her, but her stomach was tied up in knots as she waited for his formal declaration.

"How is your mother?" she asked, striving to calm her racing heart.

Stephen's face clouded. "The storm the other night unnerved her. She's not looking forward to the winter months."

Elizabeth nodded. She knew Lucy Jones' fear of high winds and rough waters. Ever since her husband had died, the seasonal storms were a frightening reminder of her devastating loss.

"She must be glad to have you at home to comfort her," Elizabeth said.

"Aye. But she'll have to get used to comforting herself, soon enough. I won't be around forever."

He smiled at her, and Elizabeth's breath caught in her chest. Was this it? Was Stephen implying that they would be married and in a home of their own this winter?

The silence stretched between them as Elizabeth waited for him to continue. Her heart was beating so loudly she felt sure Stephen could hear it. He reached up and tucked an errant lock of hair behind her ear, dragging his thumb down to her chin. She shivered beneath his touch.

"I best be getting home," he murmured, his eyes on her lips.

Surprised, Elizabeth opened her mouth to ask him why. She shut it again quickly, realizing how awkward that question would be. He chuckled at her response.

"Unless you've reconsidered?"

"Reconsidered?"

"About the kiss."

"Oh! I... I thought you wanted a kiss for your birthday," she hedged.

He shrugged. "I wouldn't mind claiming that gift a bit early."

Elizabeth laughed, and Stephen drew her into his arms. "Not until you speak with my father," she breathed, resting her head on his shoulder.

He chuckled and pressed his lips to the top of her head. "Until next week, then," he said, pulling away. His eyes were dancing, and Elizabeth's stomach fluttered.

"Next week," she murmured, blushing.

Stephen waved and started down the path as Elizabeth wrapped her arms around the baluster. She watched until his dark silhouette melted into the night.

Chapter 4

The rest of the week passed in a blur. When she was not helping in her father's shop, Elizabeth was bent over her needlework, frantically trying to finish the coat in time for Stephen's birthday. She had only two more days to complete it, and she wanted it to be perfect.

Stephen must have been busy with his own preparations, for she had not seen him since the night he spoke with her father. Usually, if a day or two went by that Elizabeth did not meet him down on the shore, he would stop by to see how she got along. But he had not, and though it may have concerned Elizabeth at any other time, for once she was glad of his absence.

Finally, on the night before Stephen's birthday, Elizabeth finished the coat. She showed it to her mother and father, who complimented her handiwork and admired the finished product.

"I think Jones will be mighty pleased with it," her father said, slipping it on. It hung loosely around his shoulders, and there was ample room for a broader chest beneath the buttons. Elizabeth sighed in relief.

"Will you be meeting Stephen tomorrow evening, then?" her

mother asked.

"I think so," Elizabeth answered. "But we have not seen each other all week, so I am not sure."

"I imagine he's been busy with other things," her father replied, settling down in his favorite chair with a book.

Elizabeth's insides gave a nervous lurch at his words, and though she was tired, she did not sleep well. She awoke the next morning with a trembling stomach. It was Stephen's birthday, and if her assumptions were correct, they would be officially engaged by nightfall. Her heart stuttered in her chest as she thought of the conversation to come, and she dressed quickly, anxious to get her mind on other things.

"Good morning, my dear," her mother said as Elizabeth entered the kitchen. Mary took in the dark circles under her eyes and frowned. "Are you feeling well?"

"I am a bit tired, Mama, that is all. I did not sleep well."

"I am sorry to hear it. Here, have some breakfast before it gets cold. Your father has left for the store already."

They ate in silence for several minutes, the only sound the clinking of their forks and knives and the clatter of the teacups on their saucers.

"Do you know when you'll be meeting Stephen today?" her mother asked.

"I imagine I shall meet him down by the seashore after six, as usual." Elizabeth could not stop the color rising in her cheeks as she said it, but her mother merely nodded.

"Just so. Only be sure to be home by dark – and ask Stephen if he would like to stay for supper."

Although the prior week had positively flown by, the rest of the morning crawled. Elizabeth tried any number of things to occupy her mind, but nothing held her attention for long. She sat down to work on her embroidery, only to find herself unpicking the random stitches she placed without realizing what she was doing. More than once she picked up a book, but her eyes would not focus, and after ten minutes she could not recall a single thing she had read. At last her mother sent her over to the store.

"Goodness knows your father can use the help," she scolded. "And heaven help me, I cannot stand another minute of your fidgeting – you are making me nervous."

Elizabeth took the coat with her, so she would not have to return home at the end of the day.

"Come to help?" her father asked as she entered the shop. The store was empty, and he was standing behind the front counter with a ledger book open before him, looking tired.

"Sent to help."

He chuckled. "Your mother's nerves could not handle your excitement, eh?"

Elizabeth smiled and shook her head.

"Well, things are pretty quiet around here at the moment. But I expect it will pick up again shortly."

Several townsfolk came through the store that afternoon, and Elizabeth was glad to have something to occupy her mind. She laughed and chatted with their customers, but every few minutes her eyes darted to the clock above the door. The hands appeared barely to be moving, and on more than one occasion she asked her father if it had been wound lately. Finally it read ten minutes to six o'clock, and she began tidying up the front of the store.

"Get along with you," her father laughed. "I can finish up

here well enough by myself."

Elizabeth needed no second bidding. She retrieved her parcel from behind the counter and left the store by the back door. Giddy with excitement and nerves, her feet kept trying to run away from her as she made her way to the coast.

She followed the familiar path northward for several minutes, ducking under the branches of an old, weathered maple just off the road. It was vibrant in shades of scarlet and gold, and she waded through the fallen leaves, searching for the narrow trail that would lead her down to the shore.

The quiet but constant *whoosh* of the sea became more defined as she drew nearer. She could hear the sound of the waves as they broke upon the rocks, the screech of cormorants bickering over their supper, and the faint staccato of the sand as the wind whipped it along the beach. Climbing over the berm, Elizabeth took a long, deep breath, swallowing the view.

The air was tangy, and the pungent smell of fish filled her nostrils. A steady wind blew against her face, and bits of sand stung her cheeks when a particularly strong gust buffeted her. She looked up and down the shore for a sign of Stephen, but it appeared that she had preceded him. Picking her way to the upturned tree they had claimed as their own, she sat down, placing Stephen's gift beside her. The sky was clear, and the air full of the cries of gulls as she looked out over the vast expanse of water. Turning herself so that she would see him approaching from the trail, she took a long, steadying breath.

After a quarter-hour's wait, Elizabeth was at last rewarded for her patience. A tall, thickset man was nearing the beach, undoubtedly making his way to where she sat. He had a dark coat and a cap pulled down low over his eyes, and his shoulders seemed oddly disproportionate. Elizabeth watched his approach with some trepidation. It did not appear to be Stephen... and yet, who else knew she was here?

As the man drew closer, she was able to make out an uneven fringe of sandy blonde hair sticking out from under his cap, and saw that his shoulders seemed crooked only because he had a large bag slung over his back. When he was but twenty paces away, Elizabeth heard Stephen's voice call out to her, and she knew it was him. But instead of easing the knot that had begun to form in her stomach, his greeting seemed to tighten it.

"Beth!" he called again, drawing nearer. She slid off the tree and stood, trembling. A lopsided grin was stretched across his face, and he stopped a few steps in front of her.

"Well?" he said, his voice raised expectantly. "What do you think?"

He dropped the bag and held his arms out, showing off the fine woolen coat he wore. It was midnight blue, with shining brass buttons and a double breast. Elizabeth stared at him.

"What's the matter, Beth?" he asked. "Do you not like it? Is it not a fine coat?"

"Oh, yes," she replied, forcing her lips to move. "Yes, it is very fine."

Stephen cocked his head, frowning. Shock and disappointment had claimed Elizabeth's powers of speech and movement, and as she glanced down at the bag at his feet, she felt the first stirrings of fear.

"I... I have been waiting for you," she stammered at last. "What kept you?"

"Never mind about that just now," he answered, spying the package half-hidden behind her. "Och, is that for me, then?" he asked, grinning once more.

"Yes. Happy Birthday, Stephen," she said mildly.

"Hmm," he mused, picking up the parcel. "This hardly looks like a kiss to me."

Elizabeth turned away.

Frowning, Stephen tore off the paper and string. His eyes widened and his mouth opened soundlessly as he held up the coat.

"Beth," he murmured.

"I am sorry," she broke in, her voice shaking. "It is not as fine as the one you have on."

Stephen shifted uncomfortably, but did not reply.

"Where did you get it?" she asked.

He remained silent. Elizabeth watched him gently caressing the coat she had made, unexpected panic rising in her breast. The coldness of fear spread through her body like poison.

"'Tis a beautiful coat, Beth. Thank you." Stephen said at last, looking up. He reached for her, but she stepped away.

"Where did you get your new coat?" she asked again.

They stared at one another for several moments. Finally Stephen sighed.

"They're standard issue," he said softly.

Elizabeth frowned. "Standard issue? At the warehouse? Since when have they taken to clothing their workers?"

Stephen ducked his head, but she could see that his jaw was set. "'Twasn't the warehouse manager that gave it to me. I'm no longer employed there."

"No longer..." Her voice trailed off and she looked at him

blankly. "Whatever do you mean, Stephen?"

"I went to Liverpool today, and met with Captain O'Malley," he said softly. "The coat is from him."

He gazed at her face, watching her warily as comprehension dawned. She looked down at the canvas bag he had dropped in the sand. Slowly her eyes traveled to the cap on his head, and then stared at his chest, her eyes unfocused, as if unable to see the heavy woolen coat he wore.

"You enlisted as a sailor," she whispered.

He nodded.

Dazed, she sat down on the driftwood tree. Stephen sat beside her.

"Beth, 'tis in my blood. Always has been. I was born to be a sailor."

"But why now?" she cried. "I know you spoke of it years ago, but you have not mentioned anything about going to sea ever since your father died. I thought you had changed your mind. What has happened? Why are you going now?"

"My Mam made me wait. But Beth, you remember what I was like as a lad – always hungry for adventure, always watching the sea for a sign of my Da's ship..." His voice trailed off and he looked at her expectantly.

"Yes," she murmured.

"That hunger for the sea has never left me, Beth, not in all these years. When my Da died, my Mam made me promise I wouldn't run off to sea, for she knew 'twas in my blood. But I wouldn't do it. The more I talked of it, the more upset she became, so I stopped speaking of it altogether, except when my Mam would bring it up. We reached an agreement of sorts a few years back: I promised to stay and help take care of the family, and she agreed that when I turned nineteen, I could make my own choice; that she wouldn't stop me if I signed a contract then."

"But what about our plans? You said you loved me."

"Och, Beth, I do love you! Nothing will ever change that—"

"You said you wanted to marry me."

"I do."

Elizabeth stared at him. "But I... my parents will not permit me to marry a sailor," she said flatly. "Unless..." Hope surged within her and she leapt to her feet. "Oh, Stephen! You have already spoken with my father! Has he given his consent?"

A smile lit her features for the first time since he had arrived, and Stephen cursed inwardly.

"No," he said wearily, "I didn't ask him that."

"But, you came to my house—"

"I asked your father for a letter of recommendation, for Captain O'Malley," he said quietly.

Elizabeth grew pale. "Oh."

Stephen stood, taking her hands firmly in his own. "This is not goodbye, Beth!" he said fiercely, his eyes intent on her face. "I love you. I want to marry you. And I will, I *will* marry you! But not now. A cadet sailor makes next to nothing, Beth – how could I support you? But I'm going to sea, and soon I'll be made an officer, and when I have a commission I'll come back and marry you."

Elizabeth's eyes were swimming with tears, but the look on his face was so earnest, so pleading. She shook her head, and the movement caused two fat tears to slide down her face. "Och, 'Lizbeth!" he groaned, taking her in his arms.

35

She let him cradle her as great sobs wracked her body. His strong arms held her tight, and his deep voice kept murmuring, "I love you, I love you," in her ear. But this did not feel like love to Elizabeth. This felt like abandonment and betrayal. How could he run off to sea, now, when their life together was about to begin? How could he turn his back on their hopes and dreams and plans? A tiny voice inside her head chided Elizabeth. *This is one of Stephen's dreams, too,* it said. But Elizabeth thrust the thought angrily aside, pushing against Stephen's chest and breaking away from him.

"Go, then," she choked, her fingernails digging into the flesh of her hands.

"Beth–"

"Stephen, I love you," she said, her voice catching. "But I cannot see how this will work."

"It *will* work!" he said fiercely. "Our love is stronger than this, Beth! 'Tis strong enough to stretch across the sea, 'tis strong enough to–"

He broke off suddenly, and a tortured expression twisted his face. His anguished eyes were fast on her face, which was still wet with tears. His shoulders sagged.

"At least, my love is," he said quietly.

Elizabeth glared at him, but the look on his face completely undid her defenses, and with another choking sob she reached for him.

"Oh, Stephen," she whispered. "My love is strong enough, too. But why? Why must you go away? Why can we not be married before you go?"

He groaned. "I cannot do that to you, Beth. Marry you, and

then leave you alone for years at a time?"

"Years?" she asked, weakly.

Stephen sighed. "Yes, Beth. Years. Probably three or four. Cadets must prove themselves before they are given a higher commission. 'Twill take me months to become a third or fourth mate. And years before I'm made a first or second mate. I won't have enough money to marry you and start a family until then."

Elizabeth winced. She loved Stephen. She wanted to marry him. But waiting for him for four years? Could she do that? *Would* she do that?

Stephen gathered her into his arms and held her close. "'Tis not forever, Beth," he murmured in her ear. "I'm a good worker. And sailing, why, 'tis in my blood, Beth, as I said before. 'Twon't be long before I'm made an officer, and as soon as I can, I'll come back for you."

"And we can be together?"

"Forever and ever, Beth."

Elizabeth buried her head in his chest once more. She was no longer crying, but her heart ached, as though it had been pressed through a wringer. She closed her eyes and took a deep breath, letting the scent of him fill her nostrils. It was warm and heady; the familiar aroma of salt and wind and wood. She would miss that about him. She would miss everything about him.

The sun was dipping below the horizon now, and Beth knew she must soon go home. She pulled away, reaching for her handkerchief to dry her eyes. Stephen rubbed his hand gently along her arm, not willing to lose contact with her. Taking another deep breath, she smiled bravely up at him, and he reached a hand up to stroke her cheek.

"I'll always come for you, Beth," he said quietly. "As long as I have breath, I'll come for you."

She closed her eyes, leaning into his hand. Despite the fear that gripped her heart, she knew his words were true.

Chapter 5

Mary Wilson was thoroughly alarmed when Elizabeth arrived home with a red nose and puffy eyes. She shook off her mother's inquiries and hurried away to her room, while Stephen, looking sober, bid her a formal goodnight.

"Why, they must have quarreled!" Mary said to her husband upon reentering the parlor.

"Hmm?" he replied, immersed in a book.

"Stephen and Elizabeth! They have just arrived, but what a sight they were! He was looking quite solemn, and she, from the looks of it, has been crying her poor eyes out. I wonder what has happened?"

"I expect young Jones has told her he's taken orders," Abram said, returning to his reading.

His wife gaped at him. "Taken... orders!" she stammered.

"Yes. He came here last week to ask a letter of recommendation of me. He's a fine young man, and will make an excellent sailor. I was happy to oblige."

Mary Wilson stared at her husband as if he had just sprouted wings. "You mean to say that he... and you..." She sputtered incoherently for a moment. "Impossible!" she said at last.

"Why is that so hard to believe?" her husband asked mildly, setting his book down and turning to face her.

"Why! Only because we have been expecting his offer of matrimony any day now!"

"Have we?"

"Oh, Abram, how *can* you be surprised? After all these years? After what I told you last week?"

"You told me only that you suspected Jones would speak out on his birthday – that is to say, today. But after his visit to me, I must confess the thought never once reentered my mind."

"And what, pray tell, did you speak of?" Mary asked in a hard voice.

"I told you before: he came to request a letter of recommendation."

"But did he not speak of his plans? His future? Did he say nothing at all about Elizabeth?"

"Her name may have come up, yes."

Mary was glaring at him, and he chuckled. "Come now, my dear, you know how he is! He has fancied Elizabeth ever since they were children. But he made it very clear to me that he would be accepting orders, unattached. And while he hopes to include Elizabeth in his future plans, he understands the risks involved in the occupation he has chosen. It is possible that she may yet marry another while he is away."

"And did it never occur to you to inform me of this? To inform Elizabeth?" Mary asked in exasperation.

"Not particularly."

"Knowing her feelings for him? Knowing the expectations we

had?"

He sighed. "Mary, forgive me. Stephen spoke so confidently of his choice and his plans for the future, that I thought they had already discussed the matter together."

"Hmph," his wife sniffed. "Well, I daresay I do not blame Elizabeth for being put out. If he has indeed taken orders, and only just informed her of his plans, it is no wonder she is all of a dither. I shall try to find out what I can from her, and leave you to your book and sherry."

Which is precisely what Abram Wilson wished for.

Mary Wilson, however, was unable to extract anything more from her daughter. "We are not engaged, Mama," Elizabeth said, her lip trembling.

"But surely he has left you with some idea of his feelings, has he not?"

"He loves me," Elizabeth answered, looking down at her hands. "And I love him. But that is all."

"Well, that is quite enough to be getting along with, as far as I am concerned," her mother replied. "An officer on a ship makes more than a warehouse laborer, from what I understand. So it is only a matter of time before he has saved enough to purchase a house and take you to wife." Her look softened, and she squeezed Elizabeth's hand. "He will come around, my dear, and in the meantime, we will begin sewing your trousseau."

But Elizabeth did not have the heart. Over the next few days she managed to pull herself together enough to smile at customers, and she put on a brave face when she was with Stephen in the evenings, but when she crawled under her covers at night she fell apart. Her pillow was perpetually damp from her tears; her eyes puffy and sore every morning.

Early one morning the following week, Stephen rapped on the door of the Wilson's home. Elizabeth peeked through her curtains, and upon seeing him standing on the porch, hurried downstairs. Wrapping a shawl tightly around her, she opened the door a crack.

"Stephen?"

"Beth! I'm glad 'tis you. Can you come out?"

"It is so early! Is everything alright?"

"Aye, but I must speak with you."

"Now?"

"Aye. I've not much time."

"Alright. Give me a moment."

Elizabeth ran upstairs and threw on a gown. She had no time to fix her hair, which still hung in a thick, honey-colored braid down her back. She fastened her winter cloak around her neck and slipped outside.

The early October sun had barely risen, and a thick fog covered the whole peninsula. Stephen stood just off the porch, waiting for her. He reached for her hand as she fastened the door behind her.

"Beth," he breathed, pulling her into his arms.

She melted into him, gathering strength from the iron arms around her.

"'Tis time, Beth," he murmured.

She knew what he meant, of course, and she clung to him, not wanting to let him go. Her thumb rubbed absently along the collar of his gray homespun jacket, until suddenly she pulled back.

"Your coat!"

Stephen grinned sheepishly. "I left the other one for Caleb to grow into. I want to wear this one. 'Twill be as if your own arms are wrapped around me."

The familiar sting in her eyes made Elizabeth blink. She would *not* cry in front of Stephen again! Forcing a smile, she looked up into his face.

"I am glad to see that it fits."

"'Tis a wonderful coat, Beth. Thank you."

She buried her face in his chest once more. "I wish you did not have to go," she whispered.

He stroked her hair, trailing his hand down the long, thick braid, wrapping the tiny tendrils at the end around his finger.

"I'll think of you everyday," he murmured.

Not trusting her voice, she merely nodded.

"'Tis not forever, Beth. I'll work hard, and when I'm made a first or second mate, I'll come for you."

"But what if you do not?"

Elizabeth regretted the words the moment they were spoken. Stephen stiffened, but she was surprised to hear him laughing softly.

"'Tis a valid concern, Beth. And just in case I don't come back, I better claim that kiss right now."

Before she even had time to register his meaning, his mouth was on hers. His lips were warm and surprisingly soft as he pressed them against her own. Her heart beat frantically, and as Stephen drew his arms tighter around her, pulling her closer, she could feel that his heart was beating fast, too.

The longer he kissed her, the more lightheaded she felt. Her breath came in shallow gasps, and his kiss, which was gentle at first, became more forceful, almost urgent. She slid her hands up his chest, her heart pounding in her ears as she wrapped her arms around his neck. But quite as suddenly as he started, Stephen stopped. He did not break their embrace, but he pulled his lips away from hers and leaned his forehead against her own. They struggled to catch their breath, their arms still wrapped around one another.

"Sorry," he murmured, his breath tickling her cheek.

She laughed weakly. "That was certainly unexpected. But, not altogether unpleasant," she added.

He chuckled.

"Stephen?"

"Hmm?"

"Does this mean we are engaged?"

Laughing again, he took her hands in both of his own. He kissed first one, then the other, then pressed his lips against her forehead. She closed her eyes, leaning into him.

"It means that I love you, and I want to marry you, and no one else is allowed to kiss you until I return."

She smiled. It may not be a formal engagement, but she considered his words to mean yes.

He pulled away from her and stepped off the porch. Her cheeks were flushed and her lips still warm from his kiss, but she shivered in the cool air. Wrapping her cloak more tightly around her, she watched as he picked up the sea bag lying at his feet.

"I've given your father the ship's schedule," he said. "You will write to me, won't you?"

44

She nodded, and the lopsided grin she knew so well spread across his face. A lump rose in her throat – how long until she saw him again?

Raising his arm in farewell, he turned and disappeared into the mist.

Chapter 6

The memory of Stephen's kiss lingered in Elizabeth's mind for many days. It sustained her through the first two nights she hurried home from the store, knowing he would not be at the shore to meet her. And it soothed her fears when a fierce storm blew through a week after he left, and she worried that his ship may be blown off course or damaged. But all too soon the ache that had been kept at bay replaced the giddy sensation in her breast, and her spirits dropped as quickly as the temperature outside.

Mid-October in Wallasey was chilly and damp. Thick fog rolled in from the sea every night, covering the town with an ethereal blanket of white. It clung to the branches of the trees and left tiny droplets of water on the surface of every stone. Elizabeth traded her light petticoats for thick flannel ones, and her summer slippers for winter boots.

With the cooler weather and shorter days came a change in Elizabeth's routine. Though she still spent many mornings helping her father in the store, her afternoons and evenings were spent at home. True to her word, Mary Wilson wrote out a long list of linens to embroider for Elizabeth's forthcoming wedding, and soon the pair of them were spending the afternoons stitching napkins and hemming bedsheets.

Elizabeth wrote to Stephen nearly every day. She knew from the schedule her father had been given that his first port of call was just across the channel, in Dublin, followed soon after by Cork. After that, he was due to sail across the Atlantic. Though ships sailed between England and Ireland nearly every day, she knew it was unlikely that Stephen would write so soon. Nevertheless, each day at noon, when she had finished helping her father, she trekked to the post office in the center of town. She would send a letter to Stephen if she had one, and ask if there were any waiting for her. It was not until mid-November that she finally received her first letter. She hurried away from the post office, making her way to the shore and their favorite spot on the beach. Opening the letter with shaking hands, she read the following:

27 October, 1809

My dearest Beth,

I miss you more than words can say. But life at sea is all I've ever dreamed it to be. The bosun shouts himself hoarse nearly every day, and he's not lenient with those who don't listen. But I'm learning quick and the captain is pleased with me.

Rations are tolerable. We've hit a few patches of rough seas since leaving Cork and have sailed through a couple of storms, but I've not been sick once. The first mate says I must have been born on the water.

Most days I'm up before dawn and don't get to bed till well after sundown. Except for the nights I'm on first watch, and then tis after midnight. I had a hard time getting used to it at first, but I keep myself awake with thoughts of you. I miss you, Beth. I close me eyes and in my mind I can see your beautiful face, smiling up at me. It makes me lonely for you. If I wasn't absolutely sure that you and I will make it, I don't know if I could stand it. It has made me even more determined to prove myself to the captain, so that I can be made a senior officer and we can be together again.

We should be heading into port at Boston harbor soon. I'll post this as soon as I can. Dare I hope there will be a letter waiting from you?

All my love,
Your Stephen

Her eyes were shining as she finished his letter. Gently she pressed the creases out, laughing to herself as she read it over again. Stephen's spelling was horrible, but the mistakes made it all the more endearing, for it reminded her of his humble face and crooked smile. She closed her eyes, pressing the letter to her face and breathing it in, trying to snatch his familiar scent. All she could smell was parchment and ink.

Elizabeth sighed, looking out to sea. It was only mid-afternoon, but a brisk wind was blowing and the mist was beginning to creep inland. The horizon was obscured by the thick cloud that blended sea into sky in a seamless blanket of white.

The cry of gulls, so incessant during the summer months, had become lonely and sporadic. She sat on the fallen tree and watched the frothy waves wash against the shore in erratic succession, willing her heart to stop aching. She read the letter one more time, then folded it up and tucked it away.

Christmas came and went, and in January the temperature plummeted. Though Wallasey did not often get snow, Elizabeth woke one morning to find a light dusting of white on the ground outside. She shivered. It would not be a pleasant trek through town that day.

The store had not been busy for several weeks. Now that they were well into winter, folks had most of the provisions they needed, and only ventured out occasionally to hear the news and pick up a few supplies. Elizabeth was grateful that her father allowed her to stay home with her mother all day now, but after lunch she donned her heavy woolen cloak, fastening it tight under her chin and pulling the hood up over her head. She did not encounter a single soul as she made her way to the post office, but her frigid journey was well rewarded: a letter from Stephen awaited her. She contemplated whether to return home and read it in the warmth of her room or to take her usual route to the northern shore. Feeling a pull at her heart, she turned her chilly feet down the path that led to the beach.

The stately maple tree that marked the trail was covered in tiny bits of fluffy down. The air was completely still, and Elizabeth's breath left clouds of misty fog in her wake as she trudged along. Soon she climbed the small hill overlooking the coast, and made her way carefully towards the upturned tree. The sun-and-salt-bleached trunk, which normally looked stark and white, was an ugly, dirty gray beneath the blazing purity of the snow. Elizabeth brushed a mittened hand along its surface, clearing a place for her. She leaned rather than sat on the tree, not wanting to freeze her backside. Sliding her thumb under the seal, she unfolded Stephen's letter and began to read.

21 December, 1809

Dear Beth,

Thank you for your letters. I cannot tell you how much it means to me to have your words before me, to read whenever I please. I can almost hear your voice when I read them, and though it makes me miss you even more, I'll never stop reading them. I love you, Beth.

I have settled in to sea life for good. I'm no longer tired and sore every morning, which helps with my morale. Now that winter has come, tis mighty cold, and every storm brings more water on board; water that freezes into ice and makes it slick and even colder. The captain cut some sailors loose when we pulled into port earlier this week. Some of them have been stealing rations, and others were found brawling amongst themselves a few nights ago. One of them was a junior officer, a man named Snyder. I don't know if the captain will be looking to fill his position soon, but I'm hopeful that I've made a good enough impression he might consider me for the appointment.

I wish you could see America, Beth. We were given a

few days' leave in Charleston, and some of the other sailors and myself went all over town, and out into the country, too. Acres and acres of cotton and tobacco plantations, though they are all bare now, and more slaves than white people by far. Tis a strange land.

We'll be picking up cargo in Jamaica before making our way back across the Atlantic to Portugal. With any luck, we'll be back in Liverpool by early February and I'll have a few days off to come home. I cannot wait to hold you in my arms again.

Give my regards to your mother and father – all my love is for you.

Yours,
Stephen

February! That was only a fortnight away. A warmth spread throughout Elizabeth's chest, and she smiled. She clutched the letter, feeling lighter than she had in days.

In only a few short weeks, Stephen would be home!

Chapter 7

9 April, 1810

Dearest Stephen,

I know I said it before, but it was so wonderful to see you again, even though your leave was only a few days. Your visit sustained me through the rest of the chilly winter, and now that Spring has come I do not think I will feel so lonely. There is such a renewal of life and vigor in the air, is there not? And you will be home again in only one month's time. Oh, how wonderful it is to know that!

My mother and father are well, and business at the shop continues as usual...

Elizabeth finished her letter and laid her pen down, blowing on the ink until it dried. She carefully folded and sealed up the paper, humming to herself. The sky outside her window was a brilliant sapphire blue, and the lacy white blossoms from the cherry tree below waved softly in the breeze. It was a beautiful day early in April, and she was looking forward to her walk. She tied her bonnet under her chin, buttoned up her pelisse, and went downstairs.

"Mama, I am going to post a letter. Do you need anything in town?"

Mary looked up from her needlework. "Would you stop by the store and tell your father to bring home some sugar? Annie says we are all out."

"Of course."

Stepping outside, Elizabeth took a long, slow breath and smiled. The front porch was lined with daffodils and tulips, and the last of the crocuses peeked up through the dark earth in bursts of violet and gold. Birds were singing in the blossom-covered branches. The sky overhead was dotted with cottony clouds, and the grass beneath her feet was springy and soft. Elizabeth followed the path to the main road, watching for puddles and skipping over patches of mud as she went along. She stepped up onto the porch of her father's store, just as another young lady was coming out the door.

"Why, Beth, I was just looking for you!"

Elizabeth smiled in greeting. "Hello, Rebecca."

"Have you a moment? Here, take a turn with me."

The two young ladies stepped off the porch, making their way slowly down the street. "I came into town to see you, but your father said you were at home this morning. I was just on my way over to your house to tell you my news."

Elizabeth looked over at Rebecca, who was smiling so wide it looked as if her face would split in two.

"Malcolm has proposed – I am engaged to be married!"

"Oh Rebecca, that is wonderful news! I wish you very great joy."

The friends embraced, the smile on Elizabeth's face mirroring that on Rebecca's. Slipping her arm into Elizabeth's, Rebecca heaved a contented sigh.

"I am so happy, Beth. Mother is delighted, of course, and Father is glad to know that I shall be provided for. Malcolm does not have much money yet, but his father has given him the farm and he is a good worker. I am hoping that we can be married next spring."

"You will make a lovely bride, Rebecca. Have you begun sewing your linens yet?"

A sly smile crept across her friend's face. "I have had my trousseau finished for six months, at least."

Elizabeth laughed. "Go on! Have you really?"

"Yes. I began sewing on it when I was sixteen, and that was nearly three years ago. But come, why do you tease me? I know for a fact that you are sewing yours now, and Stephen has only just gone away. How long will it be until you can be married?"

Elizabeth blushed, but could not hide her smile. "You are right, I am working on mine as well. But I will have far more time than even you have had." She sighed. "Stephen does not think we can be married for three or four years, at least."

"Three or four years!"

"At least."

The sympathetic look on her friend's face nearly drove Elizabeth to tears. She was happy for Rebecca, yes. But she envied her – oh, how she envied her! In only twelve short months she would be dressed in her bridal clothes and beginning her life with the man she loved. And not that alone, but Rebecca would not be separated from her betrothed during their engagement, either. A bitter lump rose in Elizabeth's throat, and she swallowed it down, determined not to cast a shadow over her friend's felicity.

"Never mind about me, I am doing well enough. Stephen came back in February, and he will be home again on leave next month as well. The time will pass swiftly enough, I daresay." She smiled. "I am very happy for you, Rebecca. Very happy indeed."

The friends continued chatting for ten more minutes before Elizabeth excused herself to complete her errands. They parted with equal felicitations: Elizabeth towards the post office and Rebecca to her home on the outskirts of town.

After posting her letter, Elizabeth made her way back to the store to give her father the message from her mother.

"Ah, Elizabeth. Rebecca Cowen was in here a while ago looking for you."

"Yes, I caught her just as she was leaving. Did you hear that she and Malcolm Brown are engaged to be married?"

"Joseph Brown's son?"

"Yes."

"Well now, that's right nice to hear. When will they be married?"

"They are planning to be married next spring."

Abram nodded. "I am happy for them."

Elizabeth smiled. "As am I."

She told her father about the sugar and asked if he would like her help for a while.

"No, the day is too fine for you to be cooped up inside. You go along – I shall see you this evening."

Elizabeth had no letter today, but her feet still meandered northward until she came to the beach. She took a different path, and emerged further east than she normally did. From her position on the berm she could see across the River Mersey to the buildings and towers of Liverpool. The shore stretched before her on either side, only faintly obscured by a light mist. Large bleached logs and clumps of seaweed littered the beach. Outcroppings of jagged rocks punctuated the shoreline, creating tidepools for curious children to investigate. Picking her way down to the water's edge, she searched among the sand and stones for glinting bits of sea shells. She found a broken bit of abalone shell and turned it over in her hand. The iridescent rainbow of its underside was smooth and beautiful, and she smiled. Stephen used to find shells like this for her. When she was a girl, she kept them in a small box under her bed. Now she scattered them in the front garden, where they winked and flashed in the sunlight like hundreds of tiny diamonds.

She tucked the bit of shell in her pocket to take home.

The cool spring rains passed quickly enough, and soon the weather turned warmer and the days a bit longer. Elizabeth knew that Stephen would likely come into port during the first or second week in May, and she watched for his arrival like a child on the eve of Christmas.

One morning, a tall, bearded man stepped through the front door of *Wilson's Mercantile*. At first Elizabeth only glanced at the stranger, but his twinkling gray eyes gave her pause, and she gasped.

"Stephen!"

Laughing, he strode over to where she stood tidying the tables and took her hands. "Och, 'tis good to be hearing your voice again, Beth!"

Elizabeth smiled, still in awe of the pale whiskers that covered his face. He was usually clean shaven, and she had never seen him with a full beard before. Elizabeth was not sure whether she liked it or not.

"Is it really you under all this hair?" she asked, stroking his cheek.

"Well, why don't you kiss me and find out?"

Elizabeth turned scarlet, just as her father emerged from the back storage room. "Jones!" he called. "I thought I heard your voice. Welcome home, son."

"Thank you, sir," Stephen replied, chuckling at the look on Elizabeth's face. "Would you mind terribly if I stole your daughter away from her duties for a bit?"

"Not at all. Just see that she's home by dark."

"I will, sir. Thank you."

He took Elizabeth's hand in his roughened one, releasing her only long enough to allow her to remove her apron and hang it on a peg by the back door. Stephen picked up his sea bag from where he had dropped it on the porch and swung it up over his shoulder.

"Have you not been home?" Elizabeth asked as they made their way down the street.

"Nay, I came straight here from the docks." He looked down at her, and a lopsided grin stretched across his face. "I had to see you. To remind myself that you're real. Too many weeks at sea... well, a man can get to imagining things."

"Nothing imaginary about this though, is there?" she asked,

squeezing his hand and smiling up at him.

"Nothing at all," he said. "You don't mind, do you? That I came to see you before stopping at my home?"

"Not at all! I should very much like to see your mother and the children. Sophy and Caleb must be so excited to see you."

They talked the whole way to Poulton, filling in the gaps where their letters had neglected the details. Stephen spoke with such vigor of life on the ship it almost made Elizabeth feel as if she were there. It seemed he got along well with the first and second mate, and that he continued to be favored in the captain's eyes. "I was born for the sea," he said on more than one occasion. Elizabeth smiled when he said it, but a stab of envy pricked at her heart as well.

"Stephen's home, Stephen's home!"

Caleb's cry rent the air as they turned onto the street where his family lived. A lean young boy with white-blonde hair came barreling towards them, plowing into Stephen's middle and almost knocking him over. Stephen laughed, releasing Elizabeth's hand and wrapping his arms around his younger brother.

"Och, Caleb! You're getting so tall I hardly recognized you!"

The boy only squeezed him harder, and Stephen laughed. They were still three houses away from their home, and Elizabeth looked down the street toward their destination. A middle-aged woman with graying hair came to the door. When she saw them, she sagged against the doorframe, clutching a hand to her chest. Elizabeth pulled on Stephen's sleeve, gesturing towards his mother. Stephen looked up and nodded.

"Here, Caleb, think you can carry a sailor's seabag?"

With a whoop, the boy fell upon the sack, heaving it up into his arms and tottering down the street with it. Chuckling, Stephen took Elizabeth's hand again and followed after him.

Lucy Jones was beaming at them by the time they reached her side. "My boy," she said, her voice catching as she hugged him. "'Tis good to have you home."

"'Tis good to be home, Mam. You don't mind that I brought 'Lizbeth round, do you?"

"Och! What sort of question is that?" his mother scoffed, embracing the younger woman. "'Lizbeth, m'dear, 'tis good to see you."

"Thank you, Mrs. Jones."

"Sophy is still at the bakery," Lucy said, ushering them inside. "But she should be finished soon, an' then you can tell us all about your adventures."

Lucy busied herself over the fire, filling the kettle full of water and placing it over the flames. She hauled a large metal tub over to the fire and placed a small bar of soap on a nearby chair.

"Mam, I don't have to bathe right now. I can–"

"You most certainly *do* have to bathe now, m'boy. Why, you stink worse'n Jonah must have after three days in the belly of that fish! 'Lizbeth and I will step 'round to the bakery and walk home with Sophronia while you clean yourself up."

Stephen cast a sheepish glance at Elizabeth, who was trying not to laugh. She arched her eyebrows at him, pinching her lips together in a passable imitation of his mother. He chuckled.

"Alright, I'll bathe. But be quick – if sailing's taught me anything, 'tis how to make myself presentable in half the time I'm given."

The bakery where Sophronia worked was a few blocks away,

and Lucy walked with Elizabeth back the way she had just come with Stephen. Once they were out of earshot of the house, Lucy turned to face her.

"How are you holdin' up, m'dear?"

"I am doing well enough. It is so nice to have Stephen home again! I do not think I will mind so much at all if this continues; being able to see him every few months, in addition to his letters."

"Hmm," was all Lucy replied.

"And you?" Elizabeth asked. "I know it must be difficult for you to have him gone..." She glanced sideways at the older woman, whose lined face bore testimony to the difficult life she had led. But Lucy shook her head.

"Stephen is so much like his father. 'Tis true, I do worry about him. But I worry about you too, m'dear. Lovin' a sailor... 'tis hard on the heart, 'Lizbeth."

They lapsed into silence as they drew close to their destination. Lucy stepped around to the back entrance while Elizabeth waited in the street out front, and soon she was joined by both Lucy and her daughter. Sophy's red hair was plaited in two long braids down her back, and her green eyes were wide with excitement.

"I cannot wait to see Stephen!" she said to her mother. Turning to Elizabeth, she asked, "Does he really have a beard?"

Elizabeth laughed. "Yes, he does. I fear a porcupine may have become attached to his face."

They all laughed, and Sophy took her mother's hand as they walked home. A companionable silence fell over them, and Elizabeth wondered if Lucy had said everything to her that she intended.

Stephen was combing his hair when they arrived back at the cottage, while Caleb watched with worshipful adoration. They both looked up as the women came in the door, and Stephen's eyes crinkled at the corners as he smiled at them.

"Told you I was quick," he said.

His clothes were clean, albeit a bit worn, and his damp hair and whiskers were neatly combed. The tub was emptied and hung back in its place on the far wall. His sea bag, which had been lying in the middle of the room where Caleb had dropped it, was now at the foot of his old bed across the room.

Sophy ran to embrace her older brother while Elizabeth helped Lucy put together the midday meal. Stephen sat on the floor between his younger siblings, telling them stories of the storms the ship had weathered and the ports he had visited. He described Jamaica as a tropical paradise, as hot as an oven but a great deal greener. Listening to the children giggling made Elizabeth smile. *He will make a wonderful father some day*, she thought.

They rest of the day passed in joyful celebration. Elizabeth and Stephen helped his mother finish the washing and ironing that she took in to earn a few shillings each week, and everyone helped deliver the bundles of clean laundry at the end of the day. They worked and laughed all afternoon, grateful to be together again. When the sun finally began to dip closer to the horizon and Lucy put the tea things away, Elizabeth stood.

"I should be getting back," she said.

Stephen put on his coat as the women embraced. "Don't wait till Stephen comes home again to visit, mind," Lucy said. "I miss seein' your pretty face 'round here. 'Twould cheer us up and do some mighty good to have you visitin' us."

"I would like that very much."

"Good."

A chorus of goodbyes rang out as Elizabeth and Stephen stepped out the front door. The sky overhead was just beginning to darken, and a hint of pink brushed the edges of the horizon. They walked in silence, their hands clasped between them as their hearts knit together. Elizabeth glanced up at the tall, broad-shouldered man walking beside her. Stephen had been strong and muscular when he left seven months ago, but the time at sea had made him even more so. The coat that Elizabeth had made for him was tight along the sleeves and across the chest, and soon he would not be able to button it up. The whiskers on his chin and face was another testimony of how much he had changed. But when he glanced down into her face and saw her looking up at him, the same crooked smile and shining gray eyes met her own. He squeezed her hand, and she felt it in her heart.

They took their time walking home, their leisurely pace punctuated with short conversations as they remembered things they had not already shared. But they did not feel the need to fill every moment with speech, and Elizabeth was glad. They had always been comfortable with silence, she and Stephen, and she was glad to see that that, at least, had not changed.

Despite their slow steps, they found themselves arriving at the Wilson's home all too soon. Stephen opened his arms and Elizabeth stepped into his embrace, leaning against him and breathing in his warm, clean scent. It was still the same: the tang of salt, the freshness of the wind, with just a hint of wood shavings. She wondered if he still carved in his spare time.

"I've missed you, Beth," he said, stroking her hair.

She closed her eyes and hugged him tighter. "And I you. How long can you stay this time?"

"Only two days. The captain wants to be on our way as soon as we've restocked."

Elizabeth's heart plummeted. Last time he had been home for five days. Would the pattern continue? Would he even return again in three or four months' time? She could not bear the thought of going longer than that without seeing him.

"Are you happy, Beth?" he asked softly. "You... you don't regret your decision?"

He tried to keep his voice light, but when she glanced up at him he was looking at the sky, avoiding her gaze. She leaned her head against his chest.

"No, Stephen. And yes, I am happy. We are both working towards the same thing, are we not? You on your ship, and me here at home. My mother..." she hesitated, suddenly shy about telling him. "My mother and I have been sewing my linens."

Stephen held her tighter. "It makes me glad to hear that. 'Twon't be long, Beth. I'm already third mate, so 'tis only a matter of time and experience 'til I'm second in command."

"And then we can be married?"

"And then we can be married." Stephen chuckled. "That is, so long as you still want to marry me when the time comes."

"I will *always* want to marry you, Stephen Jones," she said, tipping her face up to look at him.

"I'm counting on that," he said, brushing his lips against hers.

Chapter 8

The next morning, Elizabeth met Stephen down by the seashore. She hurried through her breakfast and rushed through her morning tasks, anxious to be with him again. Being wrapped in his arms was like taking a deep breath after being underwater. His love was life to her, and she reveled in his embrace.

They passed the rest of the day on the beach together; walking, talking, dreaming, and planning. Stephen filled her pockets with pretty shells, and stole sweet, tender kisses whenever he had the chance. Elizabeth felt giddy. Being almost-but-not-officially-engaged to Stephen was Heaven itself. He held her hand, stroked her hair, and whispered such tender endearments in her ear that she feared her cheeks would be permanently pink.

Stephen dined with Elizabeth and her parents that evening, but all too soon it was time to say goodbye. Elizabeth did not believe she would ever grow accustomed to his leaving, for her heart still broke as she watched him walk away from her. But as day followed day and week followed week, she found that rather than mourn his departure, she looked forward to his return. Stephen had been gone a total of eight months now, and already he had been home twice. That did not seem so *very* hard to bear anymore, and Elizabeth was glad of it.

About a month after Stephen left, Elizabeth decided to pay a visit to Lucy Jones. She packed a basket with a fresh loaf of bread, a jar of her mother's plum preserves, and a crock of sweet butter. Fastening her bonnet under her chin, she tucked the basket into the crook of her arm and set off.

Though only a couple miles separated Poulton from the township of Wallasey, it may as well have been the entire Irish Sea. The community was comprised of Irish immigrants who settled in the area when Liverpool became too crowded. All of the adult inhabitants and many of the older children had been born in Ireland, which meant that stepping onto the street where the Jones lived was like taking a trip down a Dublin thoroughfare. Neighbors called to one another as they hung up the wash and beat rugs out of windows, their thick brogue mingled with the cries of babies and the laughter of children. Elizabeth stepped aside as a pair of red-headed girls dashed down the street, chasing a hoop. It was a poor community, as was evidenced by the half-naked children and the mucky, patched-up cottages she passed. But the residents were cheerful and fiercely loyal to one another. Elizabeth smiled to herself as she stepped up to the door of the Jones' house and knocked.

"Why, 'Lizbeth! Come in, child, come in."

Lucy stepped aside to let Elizabeth enter. Her sleeves were rolled up and her apron was wet, and a damp rag kept her frizzy curls out of her face. Though it was a warm day, the inside of the cottage was sweltering.

"I'm in the middle of me third washin'. Sit down for a tick

while I finish things up and then we'll have a bit of a chat."

Elizabeth set her basket down on the table and removed her bonnet, but she did not sit down. "Can I help? Many hands make light work, you know."

Lucy laughed. "Aye, but pretty hands wrinkle faster." She winked. "Never you mind – I'll be but a trice."

Lucy bent over the rinse basin and retrieved a wet shirt. She turned the crank of the wringer while feeding it through, then tossed it atop a damp pile while she pulled out another sopping garment. Elizabeth watched her in silence, remembering the times as a child when she had helped her mother with the washing. That was before her father got the shop started, and before Annie came to work for them. They were better off now, but Elizabeth still remembered how hard the work was.

"Where is Caleb?" she ventured after a bit.

"He's been apprenticed to Nathan Cole."

"The butcher?"

"Aye. 'Twill make a good livin' for himself. And now, what with Stephen gone," she slapped a freshly-squeezed shirt down on the growing pile with a bit more force than necessary, "I canna afford to care for us all by myself. Even with Sophy workin' days at the bakery."

"I am sorry," Elizabeth said in a small voice.

"Och, 'tis not your fault, lassie. Stephen has a stubborn streak, and a mind of his own." Lucy sighed. "But never mind that now. Here, come with me into the back and help me hang these clothes up."

Elizabeth followed Lucy out the door and around the house to their handkerchief-sized garden. A series of lines were drawn across the width of it, hung from sturdy poles.

"You pull off these dry ones and set them in the basket – there – while I hang up the wet ones."

Elizabeth set to work, pulling the stiff shirts off of the line and piling them neatly in the basket at her feet. They worked in silence for several minutes, until the latest washing was all hung up and the dry garments were gathered together. They lugged the baskets back inside and set them near the fire until they could be pressed.

"Let's have a bit of a rest now. I'll put on the kettle," Lucy said.

"I have some bread and butter. And my mother's plum preserves."

"Mm, sounds heavenly! Your mother always had a knack for makin' them sweet jellies."

Lucy set two teacups and saucers on the table, while Elizabeth pulled out the bread, along with the butter and preserves, setting them on a clean piece of cloth which Lucy provided.

"How's your mother?" Lucy asked, spreading a thick slice of bread with preserves.

"She is well, thank you."

"And your sister? I've not heard how she's been since she was married."

"Charlotte is well. She has a little boy now, and her husband, Thomas, is a senior clerk to a barrister in Liverpool. They live there now."

Lucy was shaking her head, her mouth twisted in a grin. "Seems but yesterday that you were all toddlin' around together. And now your sister has a little boy of her own, eh? Fancy that.

And married to a clerk..." Her voice trailed off, and she looked at Elizabeth over the edge of her teacup.

Elizabeth took a bite of bread.

"Must be a nice life, bein' the wife of a clerk. They have a snug little home in Liverpool, eh? And her husband – Tom, did you say? – I'd wager he comes home every night, too." She shook her head, smiling wryly. "Must be nice," she said again.

Elizabeth nodded, sipping her tea. Lucy sat back in her chair, regarding Elizabeth thoughtfully.

"Have you promised yourself to Stephen, 'Lizbeth?"

Elizabeth nearly choked. Coughing, she set her cup down with a clatter. "Pardon?"

"Are you engaged to me son, lassie – that's what I want to know."

"I..." Elizabeth did not know what to say. She swallowed. "I love him, Mrs. Jones."

"Och, of course you love him, child! That's not what I'm askin'."

Elizabeth fingered the handle of her teacup.

"Stephen has been sweet on you from the day you met," Lucy said, her voice a bit more gentle. "And he's talked of marryin' you ever since he knew what that meant. But 'Lizbeth, knowin' the life he's chosen, knowin' that he's a sailor now... are you sure 'tis what you want?"

Elizabeth looked up into Lucy's rigid stare. "I love him," she said again. "And Stephen loves me."

Lucy leaned over, fixing her eyes on Elizabeth's face with fierce determination. "I know he loves you, lassie. But he loves the sea as well. The question is, which does he love more?" She sat back and poured herself another cup of tea.

Elizabeth ate nothing else.

Chapter 9

The circuit that Captain O'Malley liked to travel took in more than half a dozen ports in four different countries. By the time Stephen had been gone a year, Elizabeth had letters postmarked from Cork, Boston, New York, Philadelphia, Charleston, Kingston, and Lisbon. She found herself falling into a new routine, and the time passed quickly. Her trousseau grew larger and larger, and she felt a thrill of excitement for the future every time she added another bedsheet or towel to the growing pile of linens.

The winter of 1810-1811 was a mild one, and before long the crocuses were pushing up through the dark earth to announce the arrival of another spring. The last eighteen months seemed a happy blur to Elizabeth of working in the store, writing and posting letters to Stephen, and sewing with her mother. Even the murmurs that she was wasting her life and would end an old maid did not bother her. The highlight of her days came when a letter from Stephen arrived for her, and she treasured every single one of them. Every three or four months Stephen's ship would berth in Liverpool for a few days, and once he even stayed for a week.

Her days spent with Stephen when he was home on leave were the happiest for Elizabeth, and she lived on their memory for weeks afterward.

With the arrival of spring came another much anticipated event: the marriage of Rebecca Cowen and Malcolm Brown. In such a small town, major life events such as births, weddings, and deaths were shared with the entire community, so it was no surprise that the entire parish turned up at St. Hillary's for the wedding.

Rebecca and Elizabeth had been friends their whole lives, though they were not as close now as they had been as children. Nevertheless, Elizabeth was thrilled to see her friend getting married. It was an event that every young woman planned for, hoped for, and dreamed of.

Father Morrison looked more frail than usual as he officiated the ceremony, but most eyes in the congregation were on Rebecca, not the old pastor. Even Malcolm Brown could not stop ogling his bride-to-be. Though not a natural beauty like Elizabeth, today Rebecca looked like an angel. She wore a simple dress of white organza, with a high empire waist and short, puffed sleeves. Her neck was bare save for a thin silver chain from which hung a small silver cross. Her parents had gifted her with five yards of expensive French lace tulle, which had been fashioned into a veil. Elizabeth knew that after the wedding, the lace would be carefully tucked away and used sparingly in the years to come, to adorn only the most elaborate of garments. Rebecca's cheeks were rosy and her eyes were bright with the excitement that only a new bride can feel. Her whole personage radiated happiness, and the entire congregation felt her joy on the occasion.

The ceremony was simple and short. Elizabeth cheered and threw rice with the rest of the guests as the bride and groom left the chapel. The sky overhead was glowering, threatening to break open the floodgates on the happy company gathered below. Elizabeth cast her eyes heavenward, wondering if the storm would reach Stephen, wherever he was, and hoping that when her own wedding day came, the sun would shine in a brilliant blue sky.

Malcolm and Rebecca's wedding was the last event Father Morrison would officiate. He caught a terrible chill that afternoon, and within a fortnight, the beloved minister who had preached in Wallasey for nearly forty years was gone.

The week that followed was one of the busiest of Elizabeth's life. Abram Wilson was needed to help the other elders of the parish with the preparations to lay the old pastor to rest, which meant that Elizabeth was running the store practically by herself. Her mother helped a bit, but she was so distraught about Father Morrison's passing that it was better for her to stay home and rest. On the day of the funeral, Elizabeth sat on the stiff pew beside her mother and father. The entire community once again turned out for the service, which was conducted by an unknown priest sent by the bishop.

"I certainly hope he is not the man selected for the position," Mary Wilson complained to her husband as the family walked home after the funeral. "He is far too jovial, in my opinion. Such levity is not becoming a man of the cloth."

"Oh, I don't know about that," Abram countered. "The psalmist says that we must be glad and rejoice in the Lord, and to 'make a joyful noise.'"

"But the apostle Paul said that 'deacons must be grave, not doubletongued.'"

They continued sparring back and forth the entire way home. Elizabeth smiled to herself. Her parent's lighthearted banter was a sign of their deep affection for each other, and it cheered her heart to hear them teasing one another. It was something she and Stephen had always done.

Once Father Morrison had been laid to rest, the townsfolk began gossiping about who would be chosen to replace him. Elizabeth and her mother joined the other women at the manse one day, all of them working together to clean the place up for the new minister.

"My only hope is that the next priest is married," said Mrs. Magelby, one of their neighbors. "No man, however holy or inspired he may be, knows how to keep house for himself. Why, just look at the state of these carpets!"

"And the curtains," another woman added. "My nose is still tickling from all that dust!"

"I am only concerned about how long we shall be left without a minister, until the bishop decides whom to send us," Mary declared.

"We shall not have to wait long, I understand. A new priest has already been chosen from within the diocese."

"What! Already? And Father Morrison not even cold in his grave!"

A new minister has been chosen already? Elizabeth mused. She wondered what he would be like. Would he be old? Young? Perhaps he was middle-aged, with a pretty young wife and a brood of noisy children. Elizabeth smiled at the thought.

73

Whomever he was, Elizabeth hoped he would arrive soon and stop the old gossips from too much speculation.

Chapter 10

One month later

"Mama, I am home!"

Elizabeth walked into the parlor, expecting to find her mother bent over her needlework. But the selection of linen Mary had been embroidering that morning was in a haphazard pile on the sofa, as if her mother had left in a hurry. Frowning, Elizabeth removed her bonnet and gloves, then made her way upstairs to put them away. As she set them on the bed, she heard the front door open.

"Mama?"

"Elizabeth! Are you home?"

Elizabeth came down the stairs, the excitement in her mother's voice replacing her alarm with curiosity.

"Oh, Elizabeth, I am so glad you are home, for you will not believe what has happened! The new minister has arrived!"

Mary Wilson was standing at the foot of the stairs, looking anxiously up at her daughter. She continued without giving Elizabeth a chance to reply.

"Mrs. Long came to call this morning – she lives just down from the manse, you know – and she said there were *lights* in the window at dawn! He must have come late in the night, or else we would have had word yesterday," her mother continued, now bustling through the kitchen. Elizabeth followed after her.

"And have you been to call? What is he like?"

"Good heavens, Elizabeth, of course not! Mrs. Long and I went to call on Mrs. Edmonds, dear."

They made their way into the parlor, and Mary picked up her embroidery. Elizabeth followed suit.

"Mrs. Edmonds' daughter Jane worked for Father Morrison, you know," her mother continued. "And she has been hoping that the new minister will have need for her in his kitchen as well. Well, Jane has been keeping a close eye out for a sign of the new priest, and when *she* saw the lights this morning, she made haste up the hill and knocked on the back door, to ask if they had need of a kitchen maid!" Mary Wilson shook her head, as if appalled at the actions of Mrs. Edmonds' twelve-year-old daughter. But Elizabeth smiled; if it was not for the girl, her mother would have no gossip to share.

"He did, of course, which is exactly what we feared, for it means that he is unmarried. Jane ran home just long enough to tell her mother she would be working at the manse all day, and has been gone ever since."

Elizabeth turned this over in her mind. If the new minister was indeed a bachelor, there would certainly be interest among the unmarried ladies in the parish. She wondered idly again what sort of man he was, but as the next day was Sunday, she was not left to wonder for long.

It was discovered that Jeremiah Gilbert was a widower, which did little to soften the heart of Mrs. Wilson, who insisted that no man could possibly keep house for himself, even if he had been married before. He was about fifty years of age, with salt and pepper hair and startling blue eyes. He was handsome in a solemn way, and though the young ladies of Elizabeth's acquaintance may have been disappointed with the minister's age, they were certainly mollified by the presence of his handsome son, who sat alone in a pew near the front.

Curious glances and whispered assumptions floated through the congregation as the parishioners assembled before the meeting. The young man in question had jet black hair, and his head was bent over a book, seemingly oblivious to the stir his presence was causing. Elizabeth craned her neck, trying to get a better look at him from her seat in her family's pew. But just as the young man raised his head, his father, the new minister, took his place at the pulpit and the service began.

It was a service unlike any Elizabeth could remember. Where Father Morrison had droned on about the evils of sin and the utter worthlessness of man in the flesh, Father Gilbert spoke with powerful conviction about the grace of God, and the inherent goodness found in every man. His sermon was delivered with such vigor that nearly the entire congregation stayed awake through the whole of it, a feat which Father Morrison had never been able to boast. It was an uplifting, joyful service, and the lighthearted atmosphere in the room was nearly tangible as the congregation sang the closing hymn.

As soon as the final words of Father Gilbert's benediction concluded, an excited hum filled the room as dozens of conversations broke out. Elizabeth followed in the wake of her parents, who were trying to make their way through the masses to where the minister stood talking to his son in the front of the chapel. No less curious than her mother, who was practically dragging Mr. Wilson across the floor, Elizabeth was keen to meet them in person, but just as they reached the minister's side, the younger Mr. Gilbert slipped out a side door and disappeared from view.

Elizabeth stared at the door he had left from, wondering why the minister's own son was in such a hurry to get away from the church. She was so lost in thought that she jumped when her mother hissed her name.

"Elizabeth!"

Elizabeth turned abruptly to face her mother, who was eyeing her sharply. "Forgive me, yes, Mama?"

"Father Gilbert has accepted our invitation to dine with us this week. Along with his son."

"Oh, that is very kind," Elizabeth stammered. "We shall be delighted, of course."

"Thank you. I was just telling your mother and father that my son, Anthony, will be quite pleased to make the acquaintance of another young person," the minister added. "He has just returned from Cambridge, and having left all his former acquaintance behind, is fairly starved for company and quite lonely."

"I would be happy to make his acquaintance," Elizabeth found herself saying.

"Wonderful!" Father Gilbert boomed. "Until Thursday, then."

They nodded their farewells, and Elizabeth and her parents turned to leave. Usually the crowd would have dissipated by now, but it seemed that everyone else wished to meet and converse with the new minister as well, and they had trouble getting to the door. *He certainly seems to have made a good impression,* Elizabeth thought to herself. *But if his son is so keen to make new friends, why did he run away?*

"Well, my dear," her father was saying. "What do you say about the soberness of our new minister, eh?"

"He seems adequately pious," his wife replied. "Though I cannot vouch for his son yet. Why on earth did he run off right after the meeting?"

"I have not the faintest idea," Abram said. "But they shall be coming to dinner on Thursday, and I daresay we will find out then."

As it turned out, however, they did not have to wait until Thursday to discover the reason. Late the next morning, as Elizabeth was taking inventory in the back room, the bell above the shop door jingled softly.

"Be with you in a moment," she called, marking her tally in the ledger book she carried and setting it down. As she entered the front room, her eyes were drawn to the tall young man standing just inside the door.

His face registered as much surprise as her own, though he recovered himself quickly. "Good day, miss," he stammered, hastily removing the hat from his head. He reached a hand up to smooth down his black hair. "I thought I understood this was Abram Wilson's store."

"It is, sir. I am Elizabeth Wilson, his daughter."

"Oh."

There was an awkward silence as the minister's son fidgeted

nervously with the hat in his hands. Elizabeth noticed that his eyes were a vivid shade of blue, like his father's.

"I am Anthony Gilbert," he said at length, flushing faintly. Elizabeth nodded, hiding a smile.

"How do you do, Mr. Gilbert?"

"I am quite well, thank you."

They lapsed into silence once more.

"We met your father after the service yesterday," Elizabeth ventured after a moment.

"What? Oh, yes. He was a long time coming home."

"Why did you not stay with him?"

Anthony blanched. "I... er... well, to be frank, I do not care for people."

Elizabeth raised her eyebrows.

"That is," he continued, his face now flushing crimson. "I do not like crowds. Too many people make me... nervous," he finished quietly.

"Oh."

She watched him curiously as he twisted the cap in his hand.

"Is, er, Mr. Wilson here, at the moment?"

"No, my father is at home this morning. Is there something I can help you with, or is your business with him?"

"Yes. Er, I mean, no. That is, my business is not with him directly. My father only wished to know if we might have an account here."

"Oh! Yes, of course. Father Morrison had an account here, and I am sure that my father would be happy to extend credit to Father Gilbert as well. Shall I ask him for you, or would you like to ask him yourself?"

"You may ask him, if you like," came the swift reply.

"Very well. I shall send you word at the manse when I have his answer."

"Thank you, I am most obliged."

He ducked his head, and a ghost of a smile spread across his face. The effect, however fleeting, was tremendous, for it transformed his somber, pale face into quite a handsome one.

Before Elizabeth could do more than marvel at the change, Anthony Gilbert had placed his hat upon his head, and with a courteous nod, left the store. She stood there immobile for several minutes, wondering at the odd young man who seemed more nervous than a child with his hand caught in the candy jar. At last she returned to the backroom, and soon her thoughts of Anthony Gilbert were replaced by bolts of checked flannel.

Chapter 11

Abram Wilson had no qualms about extending credit to the new minister, so Elizabeth sent a note up to the manse by way of Annie, their maid. Soon young Jane Edmonds was tripping in and out of *Wilson's Mercantile* several times a week, picking up tea, sugar, cornmeal, and various other necessities for Father Gilbert's household.

It was not long before word spread throughout Wallasey that the new minister had an oratorical gift. Church attendance in the little parish where Elizabeth had been raised swelled until not a single pew remained empty. Every week, parishioners stayed after the service to speak with Father Gilbert, and every week Anthony Gilbert ducked out of the chapel before he could be accosted. Soon the townspeople lost interest in the solemn young man who accompanied his father to church every week, and whenever anyone spoke about him, it was always with a flippant, disregarded air. "Oh you know, Father Gilbert's son," they would say. "The strange, quiet young man."

The warm summer days flowed seamlessly into autumn, and the first week in October found Elizabeth hurrying away from the post office, another letter from Stephen clutched in her hand. A brisk wind had crimsoned the tip of her nose and made bright red patches appear on each of her cheeks, but instead of turning homeward, she went north to the shore. Somehow, reading Stephen's letters where they had shared so many trysts made him feel closer than he really was.

The upturned tree for which Elizabeth was bound was damp from the morning rain, but she sat upon it without a second thought. Hurrying to pull off her gloves, she broke the seal and unfolded the letter.

17 September, 1811

My dear Beth,

Your last letter is nearly worn to shreds, since I have read and reread it every day since it arrived. Thank you for loving me, Beth. You are so good to me and I worry that I don't deserve you.

We are heading in to Kingston soon and will be at port there indefinitely. A bad storm hit us last week and the ship sustained considerable damage. We've sailed through some rough seas a number of times but nothing like this. We even lost a sailor, who was washed overboard and could not be recovered. It was a terrifying event; we were–

"Oh! Hello."

Elizabeth jumped. She looked up from her letter to find Anthony Gilbert standing not far from the tree on which she sat; a book in one hand and a look of mild surprise on his face. Elizabeth hastily folded up the letter.

83

"Forgive me, I did not mean to startle you."

"No matter," she replied. "With the wind and the sand to muffle your steps, I did not hear you approach."

"I hope I am not intruding?"

Elizabeth blushed, but since her cheeks were already crimson with cold, he did not notice. "Not at all, Mr. Gilbert. I was merely reading a letter. But the beach does not belong to me; you are welcome here as much as I."

She gestured to the windswept sea before them and he nodded, looking out at the dark waves rolling off the coast. They were silent, and Elizabeth's mind wandered back to the dinner he had shared with her family a few months ago. He had been as quiet and nervous then as he appeared at present. The handful of encounters they had shared since then did not seem to have lessened his agitation, either. Sometimes he came into the store instead of Jane, though he never stayed long. Elizabeth thought again what a strange man he was.

She watched him as his gaze followed a lone seagull climbing into the sky. Her eyes dropped to the book he held in his hand. He had a finger keeping his place in the middle, and she cocked her head, straining to read the title on the cover.

"What are you reading?" she asked when she could not make it out.

He turned to face her, lifting the book so she could see. "*The Ingenious Gentleman Don Quixote of La Mancha,*" he said. "I was reading it as I was walking, which is why I did not see you sitting there until I was almost upon you."

"Don Quixote?"

"Yes, do you know it?"

Elizabeth smiled. "Quite well. It is my father's favorite, and we have read it together more times than I can count."

"Really?" Her answer seemed to surprise him, and Elizabeth saw the first stirrings of real interest in his eyes.

"Yes. My father and I both love to read."

"My father reads a great deal as well," he said, "but he has no patience for novels. He..." Anthony hesitated. "He feels they are a waste of time."

He glanced at her with some trepidation, wondering if his words had offended her. But Elizabeth merely smiled.

"I would imagine that a minister spends much of his time reading religious texts and philosophy. Reading, to him, is an occupational pastime, not merely a pleasurable one."

He raised his eyebrows at her. "Yes, exactly." His tone was surprised, even relieved, to hear her answer. "I was required to read such texts as he enjoys during my time at Cambridge. Science, philosophy, politics... it was all very dull," he said. "I like to read novels now."

Elizabeth laughed – she could not help it. A fleeting smile flickered across his face, and he chuckled. "Do you find that strange?"

"Amusing," she countered.

"My father does not find it so amusing. He and I used to have lengthy discussions over what we read. He would grow quite animated if we happened to disagree on a certain point of doctrine, or regarded various texts with different views. He enjoyed the argument. But since my father does not enjoy reading novels, we have not many books to discuss anymore."

"Does he not approve of them?" Elizabeth asked.

"No, no, he thinks they are harmless enough. To him, they are simply unnecessary and therefore impractical. But to me they are the portal to another world! They allow me to escape my present circumstances and live for a moment in someone else's shoes. Take this, for instance," he said, sitting down beside her and opening the book. Elizabeth drew back involuntarily, so surprised was she at his fervor and closeness. Her movement caused him to look up, and at once his face turned scarlet.

"Forgive me," he said, shifting away from her.

"I... it is alright," she said, her own cheeks pink. "You surprised me, that is all."

He smiled sheepishly. "I suppose I keep doing that. My apologies."

He turned back to his book and began leafing through the pages. Elizabeth watched him in amazement. Was this the same reserved man she had come to associate with their minister's son?

"Here, just here: 'I was born free, and that I might live in freedom I chose the solitude of the fields; in the trees of the mountains I find society, the clear waters of the brooks are my mirrors, and to the trees and waters I make known my thoughts and charms.' Does that not stir your soul? How can anyone think those words are useless?" he said, gazing at her earnestly.

"Beautiful," Elizabeth agreed.

A grin flashed across his face, revealing a deep cleft in his chin and a pair of dimples in his cheeks. The wind was picking up, and a particularly strong gust blew a shock of dark hair into his eyes. He brushed it carelessly away. Looking at her with such excitement, Elizabeth was stunned to discover he was quite the most handsome man she had ever met.

She sat there staring at him, until the smile faded from his face. She realized too late how incredibly rude she was being. Evidently he thought so too, for the next moment he stood up, looking down at her with solemn eyes once again.

"Forgive me, Miss Wilson, I believe I must be going."

"What? Oh, yes, me too."

Flustered, Elizabeth got to her feet. Anthony had quickly withdrawn into his quiet, nervous self. He hesitated, as if he would ask her something, then thought better of it.

"Good day, Miss Wilson," he said with a curt nod.

He turned and strode off down the beach, and Elizabeth tried not to watch him out of the corner of her eye as she pulled on her gloves. But she could not help lifting her head to glance at him as she turned to go.

He was not reading his book.

So deep in thought over the strange encounter she had had with Anthony Gilbert, Elizabeth was nearly home before she remembered she had not finished Stephen's letter. She hurried through the front door and up the stairs to her room, pulling off her bonnet and unfastening her cloak before sitting down on the bed. Retrieving Stephen's letter, she began to read where she left off.

It was a terrifying event; we were lashing everything down that we possibly could, but a wave crashed over the side and swept him away like a rag doll. When the storm finally ceased, the captain conducted a service in his honor. It was a sobering event, and my first – although I daresay it won't be my last – funeral at sea.

I'll post this as soon as I get to port, but you must know I will not be in Liverpool as expected next month. Hopefully the repairs will not take long and you will be back in my arms soon.

Mam writes that there's a new minister in town. What's he like? Are his sermons any better than Father Morrison's?

I love you, Beth.
Your Stephen

A single tear fell from Elizabeth's eye onto the wrinkled page, and she blotted it hastily, not wanting the ink to run. Stephen had been gone for two years, and now she would not see him this month as she had expected. Thinking of what his mother had said to her about being married to a sailor made Elizabeth frown. Was this what it would be like? Would she see him less and less as the years went on? Her heart ached at the thought.

She read through the letter again, pausing as she considered his question. Thinking of Father Gilbert brought her mind back to Anthony, and the curious exchange they had shared on the shore. He had come to life as he spoke to her of Don Quixote, and she had to admit that it certainly drew her attention. Most of the young men her age had no time or patience for books; they were concerned with learning their trades or earning a living. Stephen had reluctantly agreed to read a few books that Elizabeth had recommended to him, and though he enjoyed poetry, he was not particularly fond of novels. Learning that Anthony Gilbert not only enjoyed novels, but was heavily read in other forms of literature, was very interesting.

She glanced down at Stephen's letter. *What's he like?* Elizabeth reflected on Anthony's tall frame, his thick, black hair, and his eyes – bluer than the sky in midsummer – which had sparked to life when she asked about his book. With a jolt, she realized that Stephen's question had been about the minister, Father Gilbert, not his son.

She folded Stephen's letter and tucked it away, wishing that her thoughts about Anthony were as easily confined.

Stephen's ship made it to Liverpool the last weekend in November, but because they had spent so many weeks marooned in Jamaica, the captain was anxious to be on their way. He gave his men only one night's leave, which led to a great deal of muttering on board. Stephen kept a level head about it, but Elizabeth felt cheated. She had not seen Stephen in nearly five months, and she was forced to share all but the ten minutes it took for him to walk her home after supper with his family. There was a frostiness in her goodbye that she regretted the next day, but since she would not see him again for three or four more months, she was forced to send her apologies by letter.

To add insult to injury, Elizabeth was obliged to sit with her mother the next morning while she entertained one of their elderly neighbors, Mrs. Martin.

"Still not married, eh?" the waspish woman said the moment she spied Elizabeth.

"Stephen Jones is away at sea, Gertrude," her mother intervened, watching as the color rose in Elizabeth's cheeks.

"Hmph! All the more reason to be moving on with life, if you ask me. What are you now, nineteen? Twenty?"

Elizabeth remained silent, stabbing her needle viciously into the handkerchief she was embroidering.

Mrs. Martin clucked her tongue. "You'll be an old maid before long, Miss Wilson. Why are you wasting your life pining after a no-account sailor?"

"Stephen Jones is the most generous, unselfish man I have ever met," Elizabeth replied hotly.

"Gertrude, you know how it is," Mary broke in, trying to diffuse the situation. "Stephen and Elizabeth have known each other their whole lives."

"That doesn't mean he'll make a good husband. Why, just look at poor Amanda Phillips! She married her childhood sweetheart and what did she get? A no-good drunk for a husband and more brats than she can feed in a week."

"Gertrude!"

"Now, don't look at me like that, Mary," Mrs. Martin said, squinting at Elizabeth's mother over her spectacles. "You know just as well as I how true that is."

"Well," Mary said, squirming in her seat. "Even if it is, it does not do to spread such gossip around." She glanced at Elizabeth, who was trembling with the effort to hold her tongue. "Here, Gertrude, have some cake."

Mary Wilson succeeded in filling her neighbor's mouth with a sufficient amount of tea and cake as to render her quite speechless. Elizabeth took the opportunity to make her apologies and retreat hastily from the room. Mary let her go, but Mrs. Martin glared after her retreating figure.

"In my day, young ladies had enough manners not to walk out on a guest," she said as soon as her mouth was clear.

Mary said nothing.

"What do *you* think about all this, Mary?" she pressed. "You must know how people are talking."

Mary sighed. "I am well aware that there are those in the parish who think Elizabeth is wasting her time waiting for Stephen."

"But you disagree?"

"She loves him, Gertrude."

Mrs. Martin snorted. "Love is probably the least important aspect when considering whom to marry."

"I don't know that I would agree with that," Mary replied, thinking of her fondness for Mr. Wilson.

"Love is all very well," Mrs, Martin said, in an exasperated tone. "But surely you wish to see your daughter married and settled, in a comfortable house, to a good, respectable, man?"

"Of course."

"Well, then you should tell her to get this nonsense about Stephen Jones out of her head and consider her alternatives."

"Alternatives!"

"Certainly."

"And what alternatives are there, pray?"

"Plenty. What about that Anthony Gilbert?"

"The minister's son?"

Mrs. Martin rolled her eyes. "No, the blacksmith. Of course the minister's son! I heard Father Gilbert telling Mrs. Archibald he means to be a doctor. Only took some time off from school to help his father get settled here."

Mary was thoughtful, and Mrs. Martin nodded. "You should tell Elizabeth to think about it, Mary. Now, where is that cake? I want another piece."

Chapter 12

Winters in Wallasey were generally chilly and wet. The town remained shrouded in fog as November faded into December, and only when a brisk enough wind blew across the peninsula did the ever present mist dissipate. If the night was clear, Elizabeth could look up into the inky black of the endless sky, to where the stars shone like pinpricks of glistening ice. On such nights, she often asked Annie to add another hot brick to her bed, knowing that frost may very likely be formed on the inside of her window by morning.

The week before Christmas, Elizabeth bundled a thick woolen scarf around her head and trekked through town to the bookseller's on High Street. She had embroidered three dainty white handkerchiefs for her mother for Christmas, but as yet she had nothing to give to her father. However, she heard there was a new book out by an author he enjoyed, and she was determined to buy it for him if she could.

The previous night had been bitterly cold, and the ground was frozen solid. The mud on the road lay in hardened furrows; peaks and valleys of unnatural proportions, formed by the wheels of wagons and carriages when the weather was warmer. She picked her way through the frozen ruts, watching her feet carefully lest she fall and twist an ankle. Her breath rose in a hazy mist around her head, which dissipated almost as quickly as it appeared, save for the tiny droplets that clung to her woolen muffler.

At last she turned the corner onto High Street, and the faded green sign of the bookshop came into view. Elizabeth hastened her steps, anxious to reach the warmth and comfort of the little building.

A bell rang overhead as she pushed open the door, announcing her presence. The windows were misted over with thick condensation, and drops of water ran sporadically down the panes to collect in puddles on the sill. A round little stove sat in one corner of the tiny front room, which was packed with bookshelves from floor to ceiling. Elizabeth pulled the scarf from off her head and removed her mittens as she edged her way around the shelves to the warmth emanating from the pot-bellied stove. A man stood reading beside it, but he did not look up as she stepped beside him, stretching out her stiff fingers before her. She glanced sideways at him, then laughed under her breath.

"Good morning, Mr. Gilbert," she said.

He looked up with a start. "Miss Wilson!"

"I see you have discovered our charming little bookstore."

His face lit up like it had that day on the beach. "Oh, yes. I hunted it out almost immediately. I was worried at first that you might not have one, since Wallasey is so small. But I was glad to find it was not so. Mr. Archibald was happy to oblige when I asked whether I could be included in the list of circulating patrons. I come nearly every week."

"And what have you picked up today?"

He turned over the book that he held in his hand. "*The Necessity of Atheism* by Percy Bysshe Shelley. I am considering purchasing it as a gift for my father."

She raised her eyebrows at him, and he laughed.

"I know what you are thinking, but I have not abandoned my faith, nor has he." He shrugged. "I thought he might enjoy reading an argument against Christianity, since we so rarely engage in arguments together anymore."

Elizabeth nodded, though she was still surprised at his choice. "I came to find a gift as well."

"A book for your father?"

"Yes."

"A novel, or something more scientific?"

"He is not very selective," Elizabeth answered, rubbing her hands slowly in front of the stove. "But I heard that Augustus Crandolf has written a new book, and I thought it might interest him."

"Ah, Miss Wilson!"

They turned as Mr. Archibald entered the room. He was an aging man, with stooped shoulders and more hair sprouting from his eyebrows than growing atop his head. His face was lines with creases, and the broad smile on his face more than doubled the number of his wrinkles.

"Good morning, Mr. Archibald," Elizabeth greeted him.

"I see you've met my newest client."

Elizabeth nodded, smiling at Anthony again. "We have met before."

"Good, good. Have you come for something in particular?"

"I was wondering if you had the new book by Augustus Crandolf? I believe it is called *The Mysterious Hand*."

"Hmm, can't say that I have, since I don't care for Gothic novels myself. But you never know – perchance it came in with yesterday's order and I have not yet unearthed it. Let me take a look."

He shuffled out of the room again, leaving Elizabeth and Anthony alone once more.

"Have you chosen a book for yourself, Mr. Gilbert, or only the one intended for your father?"

"Only this one."

"Do you plan to select one for your own enjoyment?"

"I would like to, but I do not know what to pick."

"Well, who are your favorite authors?"

"Daniel Defoe is a favorite, as is Goethe."

Elizabeth made a face upon hearing the latter, and Anthony laughed. "You are not an admirer of Johann von Goethe?"

"I cannot read German," she announced unapologetically. "And the only translated work of his that I have read were selections of *Faust*, which I found tediously dull."

Anthony laughed; a slow, deep chuckle which Elizabeth found very pleasant. "I am sorry to hear it. But tell me, which authors are your favorites?"

"Fanny Burney," she replied without hesitation. "And Ann Radcliffe."

Anthony nodded. "I have read both, and enjoy them as well. What about Oliver Goldsmith?"

"Oh, yes! I enjoy his books and poetry immensely."

Mr. Archibald ambled back in to the room just then, carrying a volume in his gnarled hands. "Here you are, Miss Wilson – *The Mysterious Hand*, and the only copy I have. Let me wrap it up for you."

"Thank you, Mr. Archibald."

Elizabeth turned from the warmth of the stove and scanned the shelves. Anthony watched her as she pulled a book from a tottering pile and handed it to him. "*Gulliver's Travels*. If you like Defoe I am sure you will find this an enjoyable read."

"Thank you."

Elizabeth smiled at him, her brown eyes sparkling. She paid Mr. Archibald for the book and bid both men goodbye. As she opened the door to take her leave, Anthony's voice called her back.

"Miss Wilson?"

She turned to find Anthony smiling sheepishly at her. "Would it be alright if after I finished the book, I called on you to... to discuss it together?"

A faint flutter stirred in Elizabeth's stomach, but she smiled and nodded. "I would like that very much, Mr. Gilbert."

He grinned and ducked his head, and Elizabeth left.

Chapter 13

"Tie up the sails!"

"Brewer, throw that one 'round!"

"Watch yourself!"

"That's it. Montgomery, hold the line!"

Stephen tightened down the line he was holding as the rest of the crew bustled around him. The sights and smells of Charleston assaulted his senses as he struggled to knot the heavy rope. Grunting with the effort, he pulled it taught and wrapped it tightly, finally setting it in place. He stood, wiping his brow.

"Jones! You've a letter, mate."

Stephen took the paper from the outstretched hand of another officer. Seeing it was from Elizabeth, he flashed a grin and shoved it into his pocket. The letter would have to wait.

Coming in to port was the busiest time for the crew. Cargo had to be unloaded, supplies gathered, mail delivered, repairs made – there was a never ending list of jobs to do. No matter what he was asked to do, Stephen always made sure it was done, and done well. His hard work and dedication had paid off, for he had earned the reputation of being able and reliable, and the captain depended on him.

Once the vessel was secure and half the crew had been dismissed, Stephen pulled the letter from his pocket and broke the seal.

February 4, 1812

Dearest Stephen,

I hope this finds you happy and well. I love hearing from you and look forward to every letter. When too many days or weeks go by without any word, I read through your past letters and take comfort in knowing that you are doing what you love. I only wish I could be there to share it with you.

The weather continues chilly and damp, though we have not yet had any snow. I had a bit of a cold last week, but I am feeling better now. Sophy and Caleb came in to the store yesterday, and they looked very well. They said they had a letter from you on Christmas Eve and they put it under the tree to open Christmas morning. They said it was the best gift they received this year.

Father Gilbert, our new minister, is very well liked within the parish. He and Papa have become quite good friends, and the minister and his son are often invited to dine with us. This, of course, has raised all sorts of rumors about the younger Mr. Gilbert's intentions, but he and I are merely friends, for you know that my heart belongs to you. Oh, how I miss you!

Your last letter, which came just after Christmas, indicated that you have been promoted to Second Mate. I was so glad to hear it! I am sure you are as good an officer as you are a sailor, and I cannot wait to hear what this means for you and me.

Please take care of yourself and write again as soon as you can. You are in my thoughts and prayers every day.

All my love,
Beth

Stephen cursed inwardly as he finished Elizabeth's letter. How could he have been so careless? He had been promoted, true, but nothing much came with the promotion except more responsibility. Stephen had been so excited to share the news of his appointment, he had not considered what it would mean to her. Of course she would assume that they could marry now – isn't that what he had been telling her all along? He groaned, hating himself for his careless words.

"Jones!"

Stephen turned at the sound of the first mate's voice. "I see you've gotten derelict in your duties. I might have to report you to the captain."

Smythe winked, and Stephen grinned, holding up the paper in his hand. "'Tis a letter from 'Lizbeth."

"How is she?"

"I sent her the news of my promotion, but I forgot to tell her the pay 'twasn't enough to allow us to marry yet."

Smythe rolled his eyes. "Jones, you're the only sailor I know who's still sweet on his girl after two years. And the only one who claims she's still waiting for your ugly mug."

Stephen shrugged, and Smythe cocked his head. "Why are you doing it to yourself, mate? We've just come into port – there's plenty of pretty ladies down at the wharf who–"

"I've told you before, Smythe," Stephen broke in sharply, "I won't have anything to do with that." He folded up Elizabeth's letter and pocketed it, leaning his elbows on the railing and looking over his shoulder at his companion. "I've got watch. Captain's orders. You go on."

The first mate sighed, leaning his back against the railing beside Stephen and looking down into his friend's face. "Come on, Jones. Is she really worth all this trouble?"

"She's worth every bit and more, Smythe," Stephen said, glaring out across the bay.

"That pretty, eh?"

Stephen scowled at him. "She's more beautiful than any woman *you've* ever seen, I'd wager. But it hasn't anything to do with how pretty she is."

"What is it, then?"

Stephen only shook his head.

"Come on, mate – if this girl's really as amazing as you say she is, tell me why. What should I be looking for in a girl of my own, eh?"

"'Tis no single thing. 'Tis everything about her. Her kindness. Her goodness. Her smile... och, I miss that smile of hers." Stephen groaned, rubbing a hand across his eyes. "Beth finds beauty in everything around her, even in the people. She has a way of making you feel like the most important person in the world, as if nothing else matters but you."

"She sounds amazing, all right. Makes me wonder what she

ever saw in you."

Stephen chuckled. "Aye. I've asked myself the same thing."

They fell silent. After a few moments, Smythe stood and turned away. "I understand now why you don't ever join us. But what are you going to do about Elizabeth? She's expecting to marry you, is that right?"

"Yes. I told her that when I was made a senior officer, we'd be able to wed. But I don't see how we can. Not yet, anyway." Stephen blew out his breath. "'Tis only a shilling more a week than I was making before."

Smythe shrugged. "I don't envy you, Jones. A girl like that won't wait around forever. But the captain's got another year sworn out of you, at least. How are you going to tell her that, eh?" He shook his head, then slapped Stephen on the shoulder and strode off.

Stephen stood for a long time, watching the birds swoop and dive in the air above the bay. He closed his eyes, imagining Elizabeth in his mind, watching her face as she read the letter he knew he must send. It was at first confused, then sad, and finally angry. He rubbed his fists into his eyes, trying to dispel the image of her face.

Shoving away from the balustrade, he turned abruptly and made his way across the deck. "Beckett!" he called to a junior officer. "I'll be in my cabin for a short time. Holler if you have a need."

The sailor nodded, and Stephen ducked into his quarters. There was nothing else to be done but send Elizabeth the news. It would undoubtedly bring her heartache, but the letter must be written, and the sooner, the better.

Chapter 14

March 11, 1812

Dear Beth,

I wish I had a favorable answer to give you in regards to my new position as Second Mate, but as the pay is only a shilling more per week, we will not be able to plan a wedding yet. I'm so sorry, Beth. I know you must be disappointed. But my responsibilities have greatly increased, and tis good experience for me. A year or two as second mate will give me a better chance at securing a higher commission in the future, and when that time arrives, we will be able to wed.

Elizabeth blinked. *A year or two?* She scanned the paragraph again, certain that she had misread or misunderstood Stephen's meaning. But there it was: *A year or two as second mate will give me a better chance at securing a higher commission in the future.* Her heart sank into a knot somewhere around her middle. Stephen had already been gone for two and a half years... must another year pass before they could wed? Another *two* years?

She sighed and finished reading his letter. It did not contain much else. Pulling out paper and quill, she penned a reply.

March 28, 1812

Dear Stephen,

I am sorry to hear about your commission, but as you said, it will be good experience. I know that you love me and do not wish to be parted from me any more than I wish to be parted from you.

Spring has arrived in Wallasey, and every day grows a little bit warmer. As I was walking to the store this morning, I noticed tiny green leaves unfurling on the trees. Is it not the most wonderful season of the year? Everything comes to life again in the spring.

Speaking of new life, Rebecca Brown has had a baby – a darling little girl they named Marianne. I went to see them last week and oh, she is so little! Such tiny fingers and toes. Rebecca looked happy but exhausted, and I was glad to take the baby for a while and let her rest.

My father and mother are doing well, though I cannot decide if Mama is glad that the minister and Papa are such good friends, or exasperated that Father Gilbert and his son are here so often. The pair of them are regular guests in our home now, and no longer wait for an invitation to drop in. My father likes it that way, for it shows the closeness of their friendship. But Mama frets over them every time they show up unannounced, lamenting that we do not have a chicken for dinner or that she did not have a chance to polish the silver. Of course, you know that my mother always sets an excellent table, and that the silver only needs polishing once per week, but she fusses just the same. Anthony is far more lively than he used to be, although lively may be a bit of an exaggeration. He is still quite sober and shy at times, but he becomes quite animated when discussing literature. He is more well read than I am, though, so he must often engage with our fathers in discussion when I do not prove knowledgeable enough about the poet or book he wishes to discuss.

I miss you, Stephen. I still walk to our spot on the beach nearly every day, just to feel close to you. Sometimes I look out to sea and imagine that wherever you are, you are looking out to sea as well, searching for me.

Yours forever,
Beth

Elizabeth folded and sealed the letter, then addressed it to Stephen. She glanced at the date of his last letter. If he was in Charleston early in March, he would be arriving in Portugal in another week or two. She wrote the direction for the port in Lisbon, then stood to put on her bonnet and gloves. Buttoning her pelisse, she took leave of her mother to deliver it to the post office.

Stepping outside into the cool spring air, Elizabeth smiled. Even if the contents of Stephen's letter had unsettled her, she could not be upset on a day like today. The sky overhead was covered with wispy clouds, which did little to hide its clear blue hue. Daffodils nodded at her feet. Birds chirping in the trees fell silent as she walked nearby, then broke into song once she had gone past. Humming to herself, she was halfway down the street when she saw a familiar figure striding towards her.

"Miss Wilson!"

"Hello, Mr. Gilbert," she answered, smiling up at her friend.

"Are you going in to town?"

"Yes, I am bound for the post office."

"May I join you?"

"Of course."

Anthony turned and they began walking once more. Elizabeth noticed that he did not have a book in his hand, which was unusual. Instead, he kept his hands clasped behind his back as they talked.

"Do you have errands to run this morning, Mr. Gilbert?"

"No, I was just on my way back from the store."

"Oh? Did you have business with my father?"

"No." Anthony flushed faintly and looked straight ahead. Elizabeth frowned, glancing at his empty hands.

The color deepened around his collar. "I did not make any purchases."

Elizabeth hid a smile. "What business had you at the store, then?"

"Well, I..." he cleared his throat and slowed his pace. "I was looking for you."

"Oh."

A pregnant pause followed these words, but soon Anthony cleared his throat, forcing a laugh. "How silly we are! There is nothing so unnatural about wishing to discuss a new book with a friend, is there?"

"Nothing at all," came Elizabeth's quick reply. Her heart had given a strange, unnatural beat when he said he was looking for her, but hearing that he only wished to discuss a book – which was all that they ever seemed to discuss – settled her nerves once more. She sighed in relief.

"What book is it?" she asked.

"It is a new book that I have just received from London, called *Sense and Sensibility.*"

"Who is the author?"

"A lady."

"A lady?"

"Yes – that is the only identification of the author listed on the title page."

They speculated on the reasons a lady might have for remaining an anonymous author until they arrived at the post office. Anthony waited outside while Elizabeth went in to mail her letter. Having set it in the basket on the counter, she turned to leave, but the postmaster called her back.

"Hang on a moment, Miss Wilson, there's a letter here for you."

Another letter? She had only just received one from Stephen – had he written again so soon? Elizabeth waited patiently while the gentleman searched for the item in question. At last he dug it out of a pile on the counter.

"Ah, here it is. It came just after you gathered the first one this morning."

Elizabeth took the letter and turned it over in her hands. The direction was not written in Stephen's hand, and it was posted from London. Thanking the postman, she returned to where

107

Anthony was waiting for her outside. He glanced at the letter in her hand, then fell in to step beside her.

Elizabeth began walking back the way they had come, and Anthony frowned. "Are you not going to the shore?"

Knitting her brows, she looked up at him. "No. Why do you ask?"

He looked sheepish. "It is only... well, I know you like to read your letters there." Her eyebrows rose as his face flushed. "Remember the day I found you there? And we discussed *Don Quixote*?"

She nodded.

"I have seen you in the same spot on a few other occasions. But I did not want to disturb you, so..." His voice trailed off and he cleared his throat. "I am sorry. It was rude of me to observe you without your knowledge."

Elizabeth knew not what to say. They walked in silence for several minutes, her mind churning over his words. Knowing that the quiet, handsome man walking beside her had been watching her, unobserved, was quite flattering. But it was also a bit unsettling. She wondered what else he knew about her.

The awkwardness between them grew more pronounced, until Elizabeth could stand it no longer. "You are right, Mr. Gilbert. I do like to read my letters on the beach. But not all of them."

"Not all?"

"No. Only the ones from Stephen."

She glanced up at him, wondering if he knew that, too. But his face showed no sign of recognition at the name.

"Stephen," he repeated, frowning. "Is he a relative?"

"No, he is–" But Elizabeth stopped. How did she describe

Stephen to Anthony? Her face flushed and she looked down, agitated. When she was with Stephen, she certainly *felt* herself engaged. They had been talking of and planning their marriage for years. But were they really? No formal announcement had been made, and he still had not spoken with her father.

She cleared her throat. "Stephen Jones is a sailor, and a friend. My best friend. We've grown up together."

"Ah, I see." Anthony's face relaxed, and he smiled at her. "But this letter is not from him?"

"No," she answered, turning the piece of mail over in her hands and reading the direction once more. "I am not exactly sure whom it is from, though it is likely from one of my relatives."

"You have relatives in London?"

"My brother lives there, as do an aunt and uncle."

The conversation turned to their families, and Elizabeth breathed a little easier. Speaking of Stephen to Anthony made her uneasy; she much preferred the safety of other topics.

Soon they arrived back at the Wilson's home, and Anthony bid her good day. "Are you interested in reading that book with me?" he asked.

"Of course."

His face lit up. "Wonderful. Would this evening be alright? We could read it together after supper."

Elizabeth's stomach fluttered weakly at his words. They sounded so formal. Almost as if... She chased away the forming thought and smiled. "That would be fine."

"Until this evening, then."

He tipped his hat to her and strode back down the lane. Elizabeth watched him for a moment, curiosity and alarm fighting for dominance in her mind. Shaking her head, she turned and entered the house.

"Elizabeth? Is that you?"

"Yes, Mama."

Elizabeth removed her hat and gloves as she entered the parlor. "I have had another letter today."

"From Stephen?"

"No, this one is from London."

Sitting on a chair near the window, Elizabeth broke the seal and began to read.

My dear sister,

You might well wonder why I am writing to you and not to our mother, but you will soon discover the reason. The family with whom I have been employed for some time has offered me a position as their butler, and I have accepted with much enthusiasm.

"Why, it is from Henry!" Elizabeth cried.

"Henry!"

"Yes. He writes that the family he works for has employed him as their butler."

"That is wonderful news! But," Mary frowned. "why did he not write to me himself?"

Elizabeth turned back to the letter and quickly scanned the rest of the page. The reason for the relayed message was soon apparent.

You may be surprised, for I have only been employed as a

footman for a few years. But the reason for my quick advancement is that I will have to leave the country. The Mendenhalls' son, William, has established an indigo plantation outside of Calcutta, and is in need of an Englishman to help run his estate. I know this is sudden, and it will mean that we may never see each other again, which is why I wrote to you instead of to Mama. You will know how best to tell her the news.

We sail on the 30th of March. I will write to you again when I have safely arrived in India. Please give my love to our father and mother, and tell them not to worry. I have already written to our sister, Charlotte, so there is no need to send her word.

With love,
Henry

Elizabeth stared at the letter in her hand. Henry, leaving England? For India? Her hand shook as she laid it on her lap.

"Well? What does he say?"

Her mother's anxious voice broke into Elizabeth's thoughts. She swallowed. "He says that he will be working for their son, William, at his new estate."

"That sounds promising."

"Yes, it sounds as though Henry is quite excited. But, Mama," Elizabeth took a deep breath. "The estate is in Calcutta. Henry will be living in India."

"India!"

Mary stared at her daughter, her expression more shocked

than anything else. Slowly she set her work down. She stood and paced to the fireplace, paused, then returned to the sofa and sat back down. A bemused expression hung on her face, and Elizabeth touched her arm, concerned.

"Mama?"

"India!" Mary said again.

Elizabeth nodded.

Mary Wilson picked up her embroidery and stabbed at the fabric viciously. "Well," she said, "I certainly hope he takes his galoshes."

Chapter 15

Summer came to Wallasey on a warm, gentle breeze, heavily perfumed with the scent of honeysuckle. Anthony and Elizabeth were walking along the beach one morning, discussing the book they had read together over the course of the previous month.

"My heart goes out to Marianne Dashwood," Elizabeth was saying. "How horrible it must have been for her, to love so deeply and then to be betrayed so completely!"

"I felt more for her sister, Elinor," Anthony replied.

"How so?"

"She loved as well. And no less deeply than Marianne, I believe, though perhaps less ostentatiously. But she was tortured with the knowledge that the man she loved was engaged to another woman."

"But at least she ended up with Edward in the end."

"True. But Marianne found love as well."

Elizabeth rolled her eyes. "She married the colonel out of sympathy, not out of love."

"Married him, perhaps. But the author assures us that in time, she grew to love him as much as she ever loved Willoughby."

"But could she, really? They were so very different. Marianne loved Willoughby with such passion, such dedication – could she ever really feel the same for the colonel, who was so sedate and proper?"

"Love does not come in only one form, Elizabeth."

A jolt coursed through Elizabeth, and she stopped. Anthony had just called her by her Christian name. He certainly must have realized what he had done, for he stopped walking when she did, watching her gravely. His kind blue eyes stared unwavering into her own, and for a moment Elizabeth forgot how to breathe.

"Beth!"

Startled, Elizabeth turned around and saw a figure walking toward them down the beach, calling to her. Anthony turned, too. The man approaching them raised an arm in greeting, drawing closer.

By the time Elizabeth recognized him, Stephen had slowed his approach and was eyeing the two of them warily. Oh, why did he have to find her like this!

"Stephen!" Elizabeth turned and walked briskly towards him, bridging the distance between them in a few moments. She smiled, willing him to relax, but he did not open his arms to embrace her as he so often did.

"Beth," he said again, searching her face. He glanced at Anthony, whose tall frame now stood slightly apart from them. Elizabeth saw the men looking one another over, and a nervous tickle wormed its way into her midsection.

"Stephen, this is Anthony Gilbert," Elizabeth offered, trying to break the tension between them. It hung thick and heavy, like the fog in midwinter.

"Aye, the minister's son. So I thought."

Stephen's voice had an edge to it, and Anthony raised his eyebrows.

"Yes, he is Father Gilbert's son. And my friend," Elizabeth said, emphasizing the last word. Stephen looked at her face, and a flicker of emotion danced in his eyes. Anger? Betrayal? It was gone before Elizabeth could determine what she saw.

"Stephen Jones," Anthony said, dipping his head. "A pleasure."

Stephen did not respond.

Elizabeth was at a loss. Stephen was glaring at Anthony, who was at least trying to be polite. Not sure what to say or do next, she was relieved when Anthony addressed her.

"I can see that your attentions are required elsewhere, Elizabeth," he said. Another jolt coursed through her, and Stephen's eyes narrowed. "We can finish our discussion some other time." He bowed and smiled at her, offered a polite nod to Stephen, and strode off down the beach. Elizabeth watched him only for a moment, before turning her attention back to Stephen.

He was scowling at Anthony's retreating figure. She knew what he must think. She knew how it must have appeared. But she hoped he would listen to her reasoning and trust her explanation.

"I didna realize you and Gilbert were so chummy," he said. His brogue was heavy, which bore testimony to how upset he was.

Elizabeth drew a deep breath. "He is a friend, Stephen. Nothing more."

"He called you Elizabeth."

"Because we are *friends*." She did not add that he had only just begun calling her that. It still unsettled her.

But Stephen's eyes flashed, and his words were bitter as he spat them out. "And here I was, thinking that you were pining for me company and missing me every day. Seems you've been keeping plenty busy while I've been away."

His words felt like a slap to her face, and Elizabeth staggered back. She had never seen him so angry, never heard him speak to her in that way. Resentment surged through her, and before she could bite back the words they flew from her mouth.

"Well, what do you expect from me, Stephen? You have been gone for nigh on three years, and we are no closer to getting married than we were when you left. I have spent countless nights crying into my pillow, homesick for you, waiting and hoping and praying that you will write to me and tell me that the time has arrived, and you are coming for me. But you never have. All this time I have been alone, Stephen. My friends are married and have families of their own. You are gone. What am I to do? Tell me, Stephen – do you even still love me?"

She watched him silently, waiting in dread for his words to assault her again. But the anger in Stephen's eyes melted away, replaced by a look of exquisite pain.

"I... I'm sorry, Beth," he whispered. "I don't know what to tell you. 'Tis been hard for me, too – spending weeks at sea with nothing but the wind and the waves and the other sailors." His voice grew stronger. "I've been working hard, Beth. I've given up most of my shore leaves to stay aboard the ship and help the captain and other officers, hoping to make a good impression and be able to move up through the ranks. And I have, Beth, I have.

But 'tis knowing that you're here, waiting for me, that keeps me going. Your letters, your love... I'd be nothing without them, Beth. Nothing without *you*."

Elizabeth's eyes filled with tears, and when he reached for her she ran into his embrace. He held her while she cried, stroking her hair and murmuring in her ear. After several minutes, she pulled away, drying her eyes on her handkerchief.

"I am sorry, Stephen. I know it has been difficult for both of us. I should not have complained, nor questioned your love."

"'Tis me that is sorry, Beth. I shouldna accused you like I did. I guess I just..." He blew out his breath, and a tiny grin bent one corner of his mouth. "I had such good news to share, too."

"Good news?"

This time he smiled in earnest. "Aye, the best. I've been made First Mate."

The magnitude of his declaration fell on her like a bucket of seawater. She gasped. "First Mate? Really? Oh, Stephen, that is wonderful!"

She threw her arms around his neck, crying and laughing as he swung her up and around. Setting her down, he kissed her soundly on the mouth, and Elizabeth closed her eyes, thrilling at his touch. When he at last released her, she sighed and laid her head against his chest.

"Does this mean we can be married now?" she asked, fingering a button on his jacket. "Where shall we buy a house? I know your mother would like us down in Poulton, but I would rather live in The Village, near my mother and father..." Her voice trailed off as she waited for his response. When he said nothing in return, she looked up at him.

The sandy hair along his chin could not hide the tightness of his jaw. She frowned.

"Stephen? Is this not what we have been waiting for? Can we not begin our life together now?"

Stephen looked out to sea, as if searching for an answer. The longer he remained silent, the more uneasy she felt. Slowly she pulled away from him, out of his embrace, and he let her go. She shivered, but not because it was cold.

Elizabeth fixed her eyes on his face, refusing to look away until he met her gaze. Reluctantly he dropped his eyes to meet hers. They were stormy gray, darker than usual, and harder than she remembered them being.

"You're right, Beth," he said at last, his voice cautious. "'Tis what we've been waiting for. But we cannot be married. Not yet."

"Why not?"

"Because I've not been made first mate to Captain O'Malley. I've signed on with another captain. I'll be changing vessels."

She stared at him mutely, her large brown eyes shining with unshed tears. "I do not understand," she said at length.

Stephen sighed. "First Mate Smythe has been with Captain O'Malley since before I signed on. The captain likes having him in that position, and Smythe told me himself he's not looking to leave anytime soon. If I stayed with the crew of *The Dolphin*, it might be another two or three years before the position is open with Captain O'Malley. But the captain – well, he's a good man, Beth. He's been sailing more than thirty years, and he knows a lot of people. He sent a recommendation with me for another ship, the *Fair Maria*, captained by Seymour Strand. Captain Strand offered me the position with considerable compensation, and I accepted."

Elizabeth listened with growing confusion. "I am afraid I still do not understand why we cannot be married."

"Captain Strand does not sail the Atlantic. He sails to Australia and back."

"Australia! Why, that is on the other side of the world!"

Stephen nodded.

Elizabeth fought the rising panic building in her chest. "How... how long does a journey to Australia take?" she choked out.

"About seven months. Eight, if the weather is bad."

Seven months.

"Beth, I know 'tis asking a lot. But we're nearly there, Beth – we're nearly there!"

His words were like ice, chilling her blood and rendering her motionless. She wrapped her arms around her torso, feeling suddenly cold.

"And after seven months... what then, Stephen?"

"Well, I don't know," he said. "Captain Strand is ready to sail any day now. I need to prove myself to him as a reliable officer before I can approach him about bringing a wife on board."

"Bringing a wife... on board?"

"Aye, Beth. So we can be together after we're married."

His words did not make any sense. "But – what about a house, Stephen? Where will we live?"

Stephen was the one who looked confused now. "We'll live on the ship, Beth. Just like we've planned."

"*We've* planned?"

"Aye, Beth, that's what we decided."

119

But Elizabeth was shaking her head. "No, Stephen, I never understood that we would be living on board a *ship* together." She thought of the cold, and the wet, and the illness that Stephen had often described. Live on a ship? No, indeed!

"Well, where do you expect a First Mate to live? I canna very well supervise me crew from land, 'Lizbeth." His tone was harsher and his accent more defined again.

Elizabeth nodded, feeling numb. She turned to face the shoreline, watching as the tide pulled the waves out to sea, feeling her heart being pulled away with them. "So we are not to have a house," she said quietly. "Even after we are married."

Stephen shrugged. "A sailor hasn't much use for a house, Beth."

She turned slowly back to face him, seeing him with new eyes.

"It does not sound as if a sailor has much use for a wife, either."

"Och, Beth, don't be like that! You know I love you. You know I want to marry you."

He reached for her, but just as he stretched out his arm she stepped away. The wind had picked up, and it whipped at her skirts and blew tendrils of honey-colored hair around her face. "I should be getting home," she said.

"Then let me walk–"

"No, Stephen. I know my way home from here." She looked up into his brooding eyes. "I have been walking home alone for some time now, after all."

Chapter 16

Stephen left for Australia two days later. She did not see him the day after they had quarreled, and only briefly in parting. Their goodbyes were tense and full of uncertainty, as if they both knew their relationship hung in the balance. Not only that, but ports of call would be few and far between, so there would be no letters to send or receive. "I'll be home before you even got word I left," Stephen had said. Elizabeth merely nodded.

Anxious and heartsick, Elizabeth sought consolation in the only place she could. Making her way to the beach, she curled up on the sand next to the weathered old tree they had made their own. Leaning against its smooth, white trunk, she looked up into the clear summer sky and willed her heart to stop aching.

Elizabeth was not sure whether hours or minutes had passed, but sometime later she became aware of someone's presence. She turned her head to find Anthony Gilbert standing a few paces away, watching her.

He said nothing, merely stepped in front of her and offered his hand. She took it and got to her feet, brushing the sand from her skirts.

"I have never seen you looking so forlorn," he said with a gentle smile. "Would you like to talk about it?"

So they sat on the upturned tree and Elizabeth poured out her heart to Anthony, like she had to Stephen countless times before. Anthony sat silent and attentive during her narrative. Elizabeth did not cry again, though her throat grew tight and she had to pause a few times. When at last her tale was told, Anthony looked away.

"So you are engaged," he said.

Elizabeth closed her eyes. "I do not know. It was never a formal arrangement."

"But you love him."

She did not respond.

A faint smile tugged at the corners of Anthony's lips. "And here I was hoping that I might make you care for me, in the way I have come to care for you."

They were silent for a time, lost in the tumult of thoughts and emotions which the other's words had elicited. Finally, Anthony cleared his throat.

"If you do not feel yourself to be actually engaged, then there can be nothing improper in what I wish to say to you."

An alarm went off in Elizabeth's head, but Anthony continued.

"I understand that you have some very strong feelings for Stephen Jones, and I know that you have a history with him. I have no such history with you nor with this town, but I confess that for some time I have entertained a hope that we may have a future together. I plan to become a doctor, and shall be returning to school next year. Elizabeth," he said her name with such

122

tenderness, and her heart began to beat frantically in her chest. "Is it possible for us to... that is, do you think that–"

"Oh no, Anthony, please stop!" In her haste to prevent him from saying the words, she let his Christian name fall from her tongue. It felt pleasantly natural, which only confused her more.

"Please," she continued, "please say no more. You are all I have left. Your friendship and companionship have meant so much to me while Stephen has been away. I cannot bear to think that you..." She stood, wringing her hands in agitation. "If you say such things, and I refuse, I am afraid that you might go away also."

"But I do not have to go away, Elizabeth. We could be together."

"Please," she said again, her eyes pleading. "Please tell me that you are my friend."

He was silent for a moment. "Only a friend?" he asked at length, and Elizabeth detected a hint of sorrow in his voice.

"Yes," she murmured, sitting down once more. "At least... at least for now."

She did not know what made her say it, only that the words slipped out before she could stop them. Once said, she could not retract the words nor their meaning, and she was surprised to find that a part of her did not wish to.

"Very well. I have long enjoyed our friendship, and though I confess to wish for more, I am willing to be patient."

He stood from his seat on the tree. "May I escort you home, or would you like to remain here for a time?"

His smile was genuine, his eyes gentle and concerned. Looking up into his face, Elizabeth wondered what it would be like to be married to him.

"I will stay here a bit longer, I think," she said, dropping her eyes before her burning cheeks could give away the direction of her thoughts. He nodded, and bid her good day.

Elizabeth did not stay on the shore for very long. As soon as Anthony was out of sight, she slid from her perch and made her way swiftly home. The late summer sunshine cast slanted shadows around her as she walked, and she realized it was much later than she thought. But soon she was home. As she slipped up the stairs and into her bedroom, the enormity of the decisions she faced finally overpowered her. She sunk to her knees by her bedside, crying as if her heart would break.

"Elizabeth? Is everything alright?"

Her mother's anxious voice pulled Elizabeth back to consciousness. How long had she been asleep?

"You did not come down for supper. My dear, please let me in."

Elizabeth peeled herself up from the floor. "Just a moment, Mama."

Getting to her feet, she poured tepid water from the pitcher on her dressing table into the ceramic basin and splashed her face. Patting it dry on a towel, she opened her bedroom door.

"At last! I was worried that perhaps–"

Mary's voice broke off as she looked into her daughter's face. "My child! What has happened?"

"Anthony Gilbert wants to marry me," Elizabeth replied in a

tired voice.

"Anthony... Gilbert!"

"Yes."

Mary led Elizabeth back to her bed, then shut the door and sat beside her. "My dear, tell me everything."

And so Elizabeth relayed to her mother the conversation on the beach with Anthony. When she was finished, her mother looked thoughtful.

"Hmm. You would certainly want for nothing if you married the minister's son."

"Mama!"

"I understand that Anthony wishes to be a doctor. Think of it, Elizabeth! The wife of a doctor!"

"I would rather be the wife of a poor sailor whom I loved than married to a doctor whom I did not," Elizabeth said, rather more sharply than she intended.

Mary smiled gently. "I know that, my dear. But considering the position that Stephen has put you in, perhaps you should consider Mr. Gilbert's proposal."

"I thought you liked Stephen."

"I do, Elizabeth. I love Stephen – as if he were my own son. But you are my daughter, and as much as it would pain me to see Stephen hurt, it would pain me far greater to see *you* hurt and disappointed."

Elizabeth looked down at her hands. "Then... you do not think that Stephen will ever marry me?"

"I believe he loves you, Elizabeth," her mother said, choosing her words carefully. "But how many times has he put his career before you?"

Elizabeth said nothing.

"Has he given you a definite answer, Elizabeth? As to when you can be married?"

Shaking her head, Elizabeth closed her eyes. "I love him, Mama. At least, I used to. I think I still do. But what if his feelings have changed? What if he no longer cares for me in that way? I–" she tried to swallow around the rock in her throat, "I worry that he now loves the sea more than he loves me."

Mary's look softened. "If that be the case, I think you could be very happy with Anthony Gilbert."

"He did not actually propose, Mama. I stopped him, remember?"

"Yes, but his intentions were clear."

Elizabeth frowned. "Does this mean I am almost engaged to two different men?"

Her mother smiled. "No, but it does mean that you will have to search your heart and decide which of the two you prefer. And if I were you, I would not so easily discount Mr. Gilbert."

She kissed Elizabeth on the forehead, patted her cheek, and left the room. After she was gone, Elizabeth thought over what her mother had said. Would it hurt Stephen if she chose to marry another? His words came back to her as if from another life: *This is not goodbye, Beth! I love you. I want to marry you. And I will, I will marry you! Soon I'll be made an officer, and when I have a commission I'll come back and marry you.*

Elizabeth shook her head. He was a first mate now and earning quite a good wage. So why were they still apart? His reasoning had made sense, but her aching heart was tired of waiting for promises that never seemed fulfilled. He had told her not to write to him. He had not kissed her goodbye. Her fingers moved involuntarily to her mouth, trying to recall the feeling of euphoria when he had first pressed his lips against her own.

All she felt was emptiness.

With an aching head and a restless heart, Elizabeth slowly descended the stairs, thinking to herself how very complicated matters of love were.

Chapter 17

Autumn followed summer as it had for thousands of millennia. The trees exchanged their verdant green foliage for dresses of scarlet and gold, which they wore like queens until shedding them completely. The chilly, wet days of winter came quickly on the heels of fall, and soon another year was drawing to a close. Rebecca Brown's little girl grew into a chubby, drooling toddler, and though she was adorable, a pang of envy shot through Elizabeth's heart whenever she saw her.

Stephen had been gone again for six months now, and true to his word, she had not received a single letter from him. She missed him, with the aching loneliness one feels when a habit long nurtured is shed. Had it not been for Anthony, she would have felt his absence even more keenly.

But Anthony had been better than his word. He never spoke again of his feelings for Elizabeth, but he was the most solicitous, the most kind, and the most attentive friend she could ever have wished for. Elizabeth tried to ignore the whispers of gossip that floated around town, but even she could not deny them. It was plainly evident that Anthony wished to take Elizabeth to wife. He escorted her home after worship services every Sunday, and he stopped by the shop most days to do the same during the week. True, he was a bit solemn at times, and once or twice Elizabeth found herself laughing alone at a joke that she knew Stephen would have enjoyed with her, but Anthony was a salve to her wounded soul. He was a very dear friend, and she was immensely thankful for him.

Shortly after Christmas, Elizabeth found herself alone in her father's store. A freezing fog had gripped the town for two days, and not many customers had been lured from their warm homes into the chill. She was sitting on an upturned crate reading a book when the bell above the door announced someone's arrival.

She set her book down as the customer unwrapped the large woolen muffler covering her face. The fabric fell away to reveal the bright green eyes and red nose of Lucy Jones.

"Mrs. Jones!" Elizabeth cried, running to embrace her. Stephen's mother laughed.

"Aye lassie, 'tis me in the flesh. But let me thaw out for a wee bit afore you crush me to death."

A large, bulbous stove stood on one side of the room, and around this the two women gathered. Elizabeth took Lucy's wraps and placed them nearby to get warm while Lucy stretched out her fingers.

"Och, me old bones don't like this cold much," she said.

Elizabeth smiled at her. "You are not old, Mrs. Jones."

Lucy shrugged noncommittally. "In years, perhaps. But age is measured by more things than birthdays, m'dear."

Elizabeth said nothing, and Lucy eyed her critically. She was a bit thinner than when Lucy had seen her last, and her eyes did not hold the same spark as they used to.

"Have you heard from Stephen lately?" she asked after a moment.

Surprised, Elizabeth shook her head. "No, not since he left for Australia. Stephen said they would not be stopping at many ports, and that mail between here and there was too slow to utilize."

"Aye, he's right. So how long has it been since you last saw him? Or heard from him?"

Elizabeth frowned. Lucy knew quite as well as she did how long it had been. What was she playing at?

"Six months," Elizabeth answered slowly.

"They've been a long six months, I'd wager."

"Yes."

"But you know, six months is nothin' to a sailor. Some captains, why, they'll take their crews clear around the living world and back afore thinkin' of makin' port back at home. You may go a year or more not knowin' where your sweetheart is; always wonderin' if he's alright and when – or if – he'll come home to you. Aye, the life of a sailor is a hard one, but the lives of their women and children... they're even harder."

Elizabeth pressed her lips into a thin line. Now she knew what Lucy was getting at. She tried to smile but only managed a grimace.

"Stephen said the officers are allowed to have their wives on board with them," she said. She refrained from telling Lucy that she was none too keen on the idea herself

"'Tis actually up to the captain – did he tell you that? Oh aye, I know he'd like you to be on board with him. But you may not be able to join him. And even if the captain allows it, what about when the children come? They cannot tag along on the ship now, can they? 'Tis no place to be raisin' a family – what'll you do then, eh?"

Elizabeth had not even considered what would happen when they had children. Suddenly her insides were squirming and her face was on fire. Lucy nodded knowingly. After a moment, she cocked her head at Elizabeth.

"You've not been by to see us for some time. Sophy said you've been going 'round with Anthony Gilbert."

Elizabeth gasped. How dare she! Lucy Jones was a nosy, scheming, busybody, and Elizabeth had half a mind to tell her exactly what she thought of her.

Before Elizabeth could open her mouth, Lucy reached a hand out and laid it on her arm. "I don't blame you, 'Lizbeth. No one does."

Elizabeth stiffened.

"I love me son," Lucy continued. "He's a good man and a hard worker. But he's stubborn, like his father, and his love of the sea runs deeper and fiercer than most." Her look softened. "You're like a daughter to me, 'Lizbeth. I want to see you happy just as much as I want to see Stephen happy. But that doesn't mean you've got to be happy together. Love comes in many forms, m'dear. I'm hopin' you'll consider all your options, instead of runnin' headlong after Stephen just because you've a history together."

Elizabeth nodded stiffly, and Lucy began gathering her things. "I'm only thinkin' of what's best for you," she said, wrapping her muffler back around her head. When she had finished, she looked like a mummy made of woolen flannel.

"Did you need any supplies while you are here?" Elizabeth asked, though she already knew the answer.

"Nay, I only stopped by to warm myself up a bit. I'll be seein' you, 'Lizbeth. Good day."

Chapter 18

Some time before Christmas, Anthony had begun coming around every evening at about six o'clock. Ofttimes he would bring a book of poetry or prose to read aloud. He had been doing this now for several weeks, and while Elizabeth enjoyed their evenings together, she noticed that her mother and father were exchanging knowing glances more and more often. It irked her. Did they think she had completely forgotten about Stephen? She knew he would be coming into port in the next few weeks, provided that his ship remained on course. She worried and fretted over not knowing when he might arrive, and silently prayed that when he did, Anthony would not be around. Something told her that Stephen may not be as understanding a second time.

One day at dinner, her father received an urgent message from Father Gilbert, and he left at once for the manse. He did not return for supper, nor did Anthony appear that evening. When Abram finally arrived home, he dismissed the women's concerns and said everything was alright; the minister merely wished to discuss something with him. But Elizabeth saw both her parents cast furtive glances in her direction, and there was a decided twinkle in her father's eyes. She went to bed feeling dizzy and nauseous.

Early the next morning, Elizabeth awoke to find a fine layer of sparkling snow dusting the treetops and covering the path. Shivering, she pulled on an extra petticoat as she dressed for the day.

Although her father insisted that he did not need her assistance at the store that morning, Elizabeth accompanied him into town anyways. She was restless, and wanted something other than the tedious tasks which waited for her at home.

It was a quiet day for business, and Elizabeth spent most of it sitting behind the counter, reading. Every time her father passed her he chuckled, and at last she asked him what he meant by it.

"Only that you could have spent the day reading at home – why did you wish to come here?"

"To provide you some company and a chance of amusement," she replied, smiling at him. "Besides, you know what it is like, trying to read a book when Mama is about."

Abram Wilson laughed in earnest at that, for he knew all too well the constant interruption his wife's presence caused when he wished to read. She was incessantly asking his opinion on something or other, or commenting on the state of the roads, or inquiring after the chapter he was reading. The woman could not be kept quiet at any cost.

Shortly after noon, Elizabeth walked to the post office to see if there was any mail. She stamped her boots on the narrow porch before entering the small building, not wanting to track snow inside.

"Ah, Miss Wilson! Here to collect the mail, I presume?"

"Yes, please."

The grizzled postman handed her a small bundle: two letters for her father and a note for herself. She thanked him and left, examining the note addressed to her. With a jolt, she recognized Stephen's handwriting.

Is Stephen home? There was no direction written on the front, only her name in Stephen's untidy scrawl. A pit opened up in her stomach as to what it might contain.

"Papa, you have two letters," she called as she came in the back door. "Oh – forgive me," she added, noticing that he was with a customer at the front counter.

Her father waved to show he had heard her, then went back to discussing the details of an order with the man. Elizabeth unfolded the piece of parchment addressed to her and read the brief note it contained.

Beth,

I'm back in town but I don't know for long. I must speak with you. Meet me at the shore at four o'clock.

Stephen

Elizabeth turned it over to be sure there was nothing else. A feeling of unease stole over her, and she read the note again. *I'm back in town... Meet me at four o'clock.* If Stephen was in town, why had he not come to see her straight away? She frowned.

Perhaps he did not want to see her. The thought stung like a nettle.

She glanced again at the note. No, he wanted to see her. Tonight, at four o'clock.

"Beth, where did you put the mail?"

Elizabeth handed the letters to her father.

"Ah, I see you got a letter as well. From Stephen?"

"Yes. He is in town. He wants to meet me tonight."

"Back in port at last, eh?"

"Yes."

Abram frowned. "You do not seem very happy about Stephen's return, Beth. I thought you would be overjoyed! What is wrong?"

The man at the counter cleared his throat. "Stephen Jones?" he called out.

They both turned to face him. "Yes, do you know him?" Abram asked.

"Aye. Lives down in Poulton, don't he?"

Elizabeth nodded.

"Saw him just the other day. Seems he arrived on Tuesday."

Tuesday! But today is Friday! Elizabeth felt the blood drain from her face. He *hadn't* wished to see her. He had been in town for three days – three days! – already, and this was the first she had heard from him. Her legs felt numb.

"Elizabeth? My dear, sit down. You look pale."

Abram ushered his daughter to a place she could rest. Elizabeth sank into the chair, feeling at once both anxious and confused. *Stephen is back. But he has not been to see me. Why? Why has he sent me so formal a message to meet him tonight?*

The answer formed thickly in her consciousness, as if her mind did not wish to conjure it.

He does not wish to marry me.

Even considering the thought, Elizabeth shied away from it. It could not be true. Not now. Not after everything they had been through. And yet, looking back, she recalled the subtle changes the last few years had wrought. The shorter letters. The missed kiss at their parting. The constant postponement of their marriage. An aching loneliness began to settle behind her breastbone, and she took a deep breath, striving to dislodge it. It would not budge.

Stephen had been her near-constant companion for as long as she could remember. When friendship began to blossom into love, it seemed the most natural and wonderful thing in the world, to wish to marry him. She had never imagined life without him; a life alone. Was it even possible? She thought of her mother and father, and Anthony...

Anthony.

An inkling of understanding dawned as she realized that Anthony must have known Stephen was due to come home. That was why he had been spending so much time with her. He was watching and waiting, hoping his time may have come.

Perhaps it had. All that remained was to see what Stephen had to say.

Chapter 19

Stephen glanced up at the sky, then down the path once more. He pulled out his pocket watch, which had been a parting gift from Captain O'Malley and checked the time.

It was ten after four.

Where is she? He forced down his rising panic and focused on the hillside, willing her to appear on the trail. Finally, he saw Elizabeth's unmistakable figure cresting the berm and walking towards him. His heart gave a frantic leap, nearly barreling out of his chest.

As she drew nearer, he saw that her face was solemn and her eyes downcast. Something was wrong. A pang of remorse shot through him as he remembered their parting, and he cursed himself for the hundredth time for the way things had been left between them. He glanced at her face again, but even with the worry etched across her brow, she was exquisitely beautiful. Her golden hair was concealed beneath the hood of her cloak, but a few loose curls hung around her face, offsetting her porcelain skin and rosy cheeks to perfection.

At last she stood before him, and raised her eyes to his face.

They were beautiful, too – large and round, with thick, dark lashes. But their warm brown hue was clouded with uncertainty, and some other emotion he could not quite name.

"Hello, Stephen."

Her greeting hung in the air between them. Stephen tried to smile at her, but the solemnity with which she looked at him caused him to pause.

"I was starting to worry. What kept you?"

She merely shrugged and looked away.

"I'm glad you got my note. I wondered if you had received the message."

"I did." She faced him once more. "It was very good of you to send me word of your arrival."

Something in her tone unnerved him. Did she know that he had been in town for a few days already? He squirmed inside. "I've missed your letters. How have you been?"

"You told me not to write."

"I know that. But I've missed them all the same. I've missed you."

An icy wind blew across the beach, and Elizabeth drew her cloak more tightly around her. "Have you?" she asked, once more looking out across the sea.

"Course I have! What sort of question is that?" His concern was swiftly turning to fear, which made him respond in anger. *She acts as if she didna even miss me. As if...*

His eyes narrowed. "Tell me, how is Anthony Gilbert faring?"

The tone of his voice caused Elizabeth to turn. He was obviously angry, but looking into his face, Elizabeth could see fear and pain as well.

Elizabeth closed her eyes. "What do you want from me, Stephen? Tell me so at once so that I might return home."

"Are you saying that you only came because I asked you to come?"

"Of course. I did not even know you were in town. As I said, it was good of you to inform me of your arrival on Tuesday."

Her caustic look made Stephen freeze. "Who told you I've been in town since Tuesday?"

"Does it matter? You have been home for three days, Stephen, and you never once came to call. Why? Why have you not come to see me?"

"I've had... business to take care of."

Pain slashed at Elizabeth's heart. "Business? You have been gone for seven months, and you had to see about your business before seeing me?"

"Beth, listen to me. I–"

"Stephen, I believe I should be getting home."

"No!" He shouted the word, throwing it across the emptiness between them. "I'll not let you go, Beth. Not back home. Not back to him."

She paused. "Back to him?"

"Gilbert. The minister's son."

Elizabeth could see the effort he made to keep the bitterness out of his voice, but it crept in all the same. Did he honestly think she preferred Anthony's company to his own?

"Anthony has been a good friend to me, Stephen," she said quietly.

"A friend."

"Yes, a *friend*. You have been gone, Stephen. For more than three years I have been alone. And every time you received a promotion and I thought we could be together, you have made excuses. I love you Stephen, but it seems as if your love for the sea has overpowered the love you used to have for me."

Staring up into his face, Elizabeth's breath caught. He was taller than she remembered, and his face was clean shaven once more. She had grown accustomed to his beard, and seeing his boyish face brought back all the memories they had made together, all the years they had planned. She bit her lip and turned away, fighting back the tears that threatened to overflow. Being with him again brought all her feelings crashing back into her heart, and if she did not leave soon she was afraid she might fall apart.

"You... you still love me?"

Stephen's voice was quiet, and he asked the question as if he dared not hear the answer. Elizabeth glared at him, confused.

"Of course I love you. Do you think I–"

But she did not finish. In one move Stephen had cupped her face in his hands and pressed his mouth against hers. Elizabeth barely had time to catch her breath. He kissed her as he had never kissed her before, as if he were afraid she might disappear out of his arms at any moment. His hands slid down her neck and across her shoulders, brushing along her arms as he reached under her cloak to put his arms around her waist. Elizabeth trembled. His lips moved in unison with hers and he pulled her close, pressing her body against his.

The anger, disappointment, and heartache Elizabeth felt seemed to melt away as Stephen kissed her. All she knew was the softness of his lips, the warmth of his body, the strength of his arms. Her hands slid up his chest and wrapped themselves around his neck. She reached her fingers up and ran them through his hair as his lips moved to the corner of her mouth and then down her jawline. She shivered, closing her eyes.

"Elizabeth." His breath tickled her cheek as he murmured in her ear. "You have no idea the madness I've felt, the fear that has consumed me these last several months." He pulled back and rested his forehead against hers, reaching his hands up to cup her face once more. "When last we met... when I saw you with *him*..." His voice trailed off and he shook his head. "I was afraid I'd be too late. That you'd have already given your heart to him."

"Never," Elizabeth whispered. "My heart has always belonged to you, Stephen Jones."

"Och, I'm glad to hear it. But Beth, about the house..."

"It is alright, Stephen, I understand."

"No, I need to apologize. It was selfish and insensitive of me to dismiss your concerns. Of course we can buy a house, in The Village, near your folks, if you'd like."

Elizabeth drew back, confused. "What about your commission? You said a sailor has no need for a house."

"Aye, 'tis true. But I'm willing to give up the sea, and my commission, if that's what it takes to have you for my bride."

"You... what?"

Stephen swallowed. "I've taken a leave of absence. Two months. I didn't want to resign outright in case... well, in case you wouldn't have me."

Elizabeth closed her eyes.

"But knowing now that you're still here, and that you still love me, well, two months should be enough time to find a place of our own and settle down. I'll do my best to find work. I'll go back–"

"Stephen."

"–to the warehouses and ask the foreman if–"

"Stephen!"

He paused, looking anxiously into her face, and she stood up on her tiptoes to kiss him. He relaxed, wrapping his arms around her again.

"Stephen, I cannot even express how happy I am to hear those words. But I do not want you to give up something you love as much as the sea."

"I love you more, Beth."

She smiled. "I know that now, and oh, how glad it makes me! But you would not be happy. And neither would I, knowing how much you would miss it."

Stephen swallowed, nodding. Elizabeth leaned her head against his chest, looking out to sea. "Why did you not call for me on Tuesday?"

Stephen laughed self-consciously. "I meant to go about it the right way this time. So I came to town and told my Mam about my plans. You can imagine how happy she was to hear I might give up the sea." He shook his head. "And then I went to see the minister."

"Father Gilbert?"

"Aye. I didn't dare call on your father at home, so I went to St. Hillary's and sent word for your father to join me there."

Elizabeth was nodding. "Yes, he left for the manse on urgent business earlier this week."

"I asked him for your hand, and he said yes."

Elizabeth exhaled, smiling to herself.

"Then I asked Father Gilbert if he would marry us. He agreed to do so whenever we'd like, once I procure a license."

Suddenly Elizabeth gasped, pulling back to look at him. "Was Anthony there? Did he see and hear you?" Her stomach felt like lead at the thought. But Stephen shook his head.

"No, he wasn't there. I'm sure Father Gilbert told him the news, though."

Elizabeth sagged against Stephen's chest. "Yes, you are probably right. I have not seen him all week."

Her heart ached. Though she never meant to hurt him, she could not help but feel that she was somehow to blame for the pain he must feel. The minutes ticked by, marked by the undulating waves near their feet. At last Stephen broke the silence.

"Do you have regrets, 'Lizbeth?" he asked softly. "About Anthony?"

Elizabeth shook her head. "No. He is my friend, Stephen – but nothing more. I am sorry to have caused him pain, but I do not regret him."

They were quiet again, and Stephen breathed more easily. "Tell me about Australia," Elizabeth said at length.

"'Tis a strange land, Beth. Hot, and dry. Some of the funniest creatures you ever saw, and the way the people talk?" He chuckled. "Makes me wonder if they really come from England."

Elizabeth smiled. "I want to see it. I want to see Australia. And Jamaica. And Africa. And everywhere else you have been."

Stepping back to look into her face, Stephen frowned. "Are you sure, Beth? Is that really what you want?"

She nodded. "Yes, Stephen. I want to be with you. I want to see the things that you have seen; all those wonderful places I have visited only in your letters."

"I've been a selfish beast, Beth. Only thinking of what I want and what will make me happy. Going off to sea. Bringing you along with me... Those have been my dreams, Beth. What about your dreams?"

"*You* are my dream, Stephen," she said, twining her fingers into his.

He kissed the tip of her nose. "We can still get a house if you like, Beth. I may not be there very often, but you might like to have a place to call home."

Elizabeth reached up and brushed an errant lock of hair away from his forehead. "You are my home," she said.

Stephen grinned, and kissed her again.

Epilogue

Elizabeth drew her cloak more tightly around her neck. The icy wind bit into her nose and cheeks, nipping at her ankles as her skirts swirled around her. The dock was slick and damp beneath her feet, and if it had not been for the tight grip Stephen maintained on her elbow, she felt sure she would have fallen.

They walked up the gangplank together; Elizabeth clutching the small valise that had once belonged to her mother, and Stephen carrying her large trunk up on his opposite shoulder. She glanced sideways at her husband and smiled. He was far more muscular than she remembered him being, and now she knew why.

They reached the deck of the ship and Stephen released his hold on her. "I'll stow these things in the cabin and be back to give you a tour. Wait for me here."

She gave him her valise, and he strode off carrying the luggage. Dozens of sailors bustled about, making the final preparations before embarking on their long journey to the other side of the world. The ship would be leaving any moment. A lone gull flew overhead, and she watched as it fought against the wind. Suddenly she heard a voice calling her name. Turning back towards the dock, she looked straight into the eyes of Anthony Gilbert.

For a moment, neither of them moved. Then Anthony smiled. Relief coursed through Elizabeth's veins, and she turned to go down the gangplank once more.

"Ma'am, you shouldn't leave the ship – captain's orders are to–"

"I shall only be a moment," she said to the sailor standing watch, who frowned but let her pass. She picked her way back down the ramp to where Anthony stood on the wharf.

They had not spoken since before Stephen's arrival, and the only time Elizabeth had seen him since then was at church, and only from a distance. The moment the service had ended, Anthony had ducked out a side door, exactly as he had when he first came to Wallasey. She was glad to see him, though she knew not what she could possibly say.

"I felt I ought to say goodbye before you left," he said when she was standing before him.

"I am glad that you came."

The silence stretched between them: an ocean of questions and unspoken explanations.

"Anthony," Elizabeth began at length. "I want you to know that–"

"Please, Elizabeth – Mrs. Jones – you owe me no explanation." He smiled a little wistfully. "You were very honest with me. I knew your feelings all along."

She nodded, a lump rising in her throat. "Thank you, Anthony, for your friendship. I sincerely wish you all that may contribute to your future happiness."

"And I you."

"Thank you."

When nothing more was said, Elizabeth turned to climb to the deck of the ship. Glancing up the gangplank, she saw Stephen, watching her. As she made her way towards him, his eyes slid from her face to the man she had been speaking to.

A harsh cry and a shrill whistle rent the air, and as soon as Elizabeth had mounted the deck the gangplank was drawn. Anthony and Stephen were still staring at one another. Then, slowly, Stephen raised his arm in farewell.

Elizabeth watched as Anthony returned the gesture. Stephen turned and barked an order to a couple of sailors, then took Elizabeth by the arm.

"Beth, 'tis time to go."

She nodded, and followed him as he led her to the bow of the ship. The smaller sails were unfurled and they were immediately filled by the wind, drawing the ship away from the dock and out of the harbor. Stephen watched Elizabeth's face with concern.

"Are you ready to say goodbye?" he asked, his gray eyes full of questions.

Elizabeth looked out across the open water and took a deep breath. The tang of salt and wind and adventure bit into her nostrils. She smiled up at Stephen.

"No," she said. "I am ready to embrace what comes."

About the Author

 Shaela Kay was born and raised near Seattle, Washington. She studied Theatre and English at Brigham Young University-Idaho, but left her studies in order to be a wife and a mother. When she isn't writing, you can find her quilting, crafting, or homeschooling her four children. She and her husband John live with their family in a little house along the banks of the mighty Columbia River. Visit her online at www.shaelakay.com.